HEARTBREAK CABIN

LIFE ON THE ALASKA FRONTIER

I0628620

G.E. SHERMAN

Heartbreak Cabin

ISBN-13: 978-0998547794

This work is historical fiction. Some of the incidents described herein may not exactly align with actual events of the period. All the characters in this book are fictional.

FLEETING EDGE PRESS, 2020

*To Christina and Gregory, of whom I could not
be more proud.*

"A mine is a hole in the ground into which heart, soul, and fortune are poured in hopes of gaining a bit of shiny metal."
Thomas Everton Thornton

For gold is tried in the fire and acceptable men in the furnace of adversity.
George Santayana

The refining pot is for silver and the furnace for gold, but the LORD tests the hearts.
Proverbs 17:3

Books in the
Life on the Alaska Frontier **series**

I. FORGING NORTH

II. FORTYMILE

III. HEARTBREAK CABIN

CONTENTS

Chapter 1   1

Chapter 2   7

Chapter 3   11

Chapter 4   17

Chapter 5   23

Chapter 6   29

Chapter 7   37

Chapter 8   47

Chapter 9   57

Chapter 10   71

Chapter 11   81

Chapter 12   89

Chapter 13   107

Chapter 14   117

Chapter 15   131

Chapter 16   145

Chapter 17   155

Chapter 18   167

Chapter 19	**183**
Chapter 20	**195**
Chapter 21	**205**
Chapter 22	**215**
Chapter 23	**225**
Chapter 24	**239**
Epilogue	**251**
Glossary of Terms	**253**
About the Author	**255**

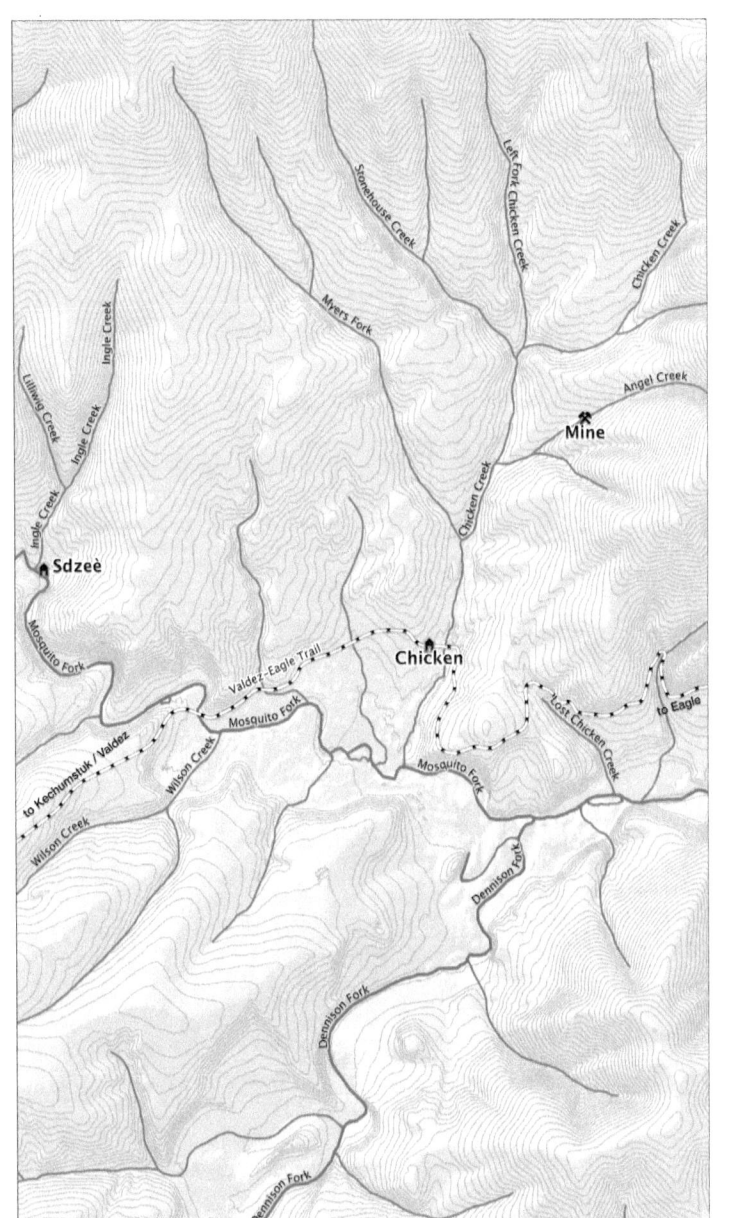

CHAPTER 1

The sun glistened off the snow-covered river, frozen in time, at least for a season. Despite the days growing longer, the temperatures remained below freezing. In vain, the sun struggled to loosen winter's grip. Thomas Thornton shuffled along the trapline, hoping to have more success today.

It was a welcome relief from mining frozen gravel, spending all day underground, hauling bucket after bucket topside, then building a fire for the nightly thaw.

Not being able to see the fruits of his labor was frustrating—it was impossible to process the gravel in the winter. The only gold he recovered was the little bit panned using a hole chopped in the ice on Angel Creek.

I can't wait for spring, he thought.

The trapline yielded some fur, mostly marten and lynx, along with a single wolverine. The sets among the dwarf spruce were easy to keep up—beaver trapping was another matter entirely. The severe winter temperatures easily froze the river and ponds three feet or more thick. Chopping through it to create a beaver set took a lot of time, and with each night, the hole refroze, making checking of the traps more of a chore. At times the new ice was clear enough to see if he caught something. At other times, it's was a matter of chopping the hole open.

Reaching the edge of the river, Thomas slid down the

bank onto a patch of windswept ice. Pulling the coat tight around his neck, he stopped. A touch of sadness swept across his face. Today was the day—and he couldn't be there.

The telegram from Valdez came as a bit of a surprise—John asking Stella to marry him and move north. Now the pressure was on Thomas to get everything ready, despite their arrival being more than a month away. Even so, it couldn't come soon enough—he looked forward to Emily, John, and Stella coming up, to no longer being alone. Yet, he worried—the cramped cabin was really unsuitable and it was way too early to start building a new house.

Moving down the river, his thoughts returned to the wedding, to Stella who was like a mother to him, nursing him back to health after being shot his first day in Alaska. He was happy for her, and yet being absent tugged at him, almost as much as the iciness of the morning air.

It was almost imperceptible—the sound. He stopped, turning to look as the ice gave way, plunging him into the freezing waters of the Mosquito Fork river.

† † †

For a brief instant, the image of her deceased husband flickered in her mind. She didn't know why—why the image of Wesley would storm into her mind. More than five years had passed since he headed into the mountains that day. How often she wondered if he suffered—if his end had been long and agonizing. A flurry of memories rushed in, overwhelming her senses.

"Stella? Stella Baird?"

She paused. "I...I do."

"I now pronounce you man and wife," said Pastor Burnett. "You may kiss the bride."

Stella blushed as John gave her a lingering kiss, the audience approving with raucous applause.

The ceremony at Endeavor Congregational Church was more than she wanted. Stella lobbied hard for a simple civil ceremony—her, John Palmer, and his daughter Emily standing before the magistrate. John would have none of it. Instead, he surprised her with a lavish ceremony, severely draining his bank account while betting on Thomas to come through financially. "It's about as fancy as one gets in 1900's Valdez Alaska," he boasted at the time.

"Folks, we're going to have a reception at the town hall in about an hour—see you there," said the pastor as people began to file out of the church.

"I'm really surprised," said Stella. "Looks like most of the Valdez old-timers turned out. You must have sent out a lot of invitations."

"I tried to invite everyone in town," said John as he stretched out his hand. "Shall we head to the reception?"

"Shouldn't we clean up here a bit first?"

John smiled. "Always on duty, dear?

It still sounded foreign to her—being called "dear."

"Today's your day, Stella. I've taken care of everything so just relax," said John.

The guests departed—only Emily remained up front, talking to the pastor. Shortly, she joined Stella and John.

"What were you talking to him about?" said John.

"About my wedding. I want him to perform it as well."

"Emily, dear, your fiancé is almost four-hundred miles away. I don't think you're getting married here."

Emily scowled, biting her lip. "Why not, Father? We're coming back after we visit aren't we?"

John looked at her, then shook his head. "I'm afraid you misunderstand, Emily. We are *moving* to Chicken."

Emily's scowl deepened, wrinkles appearing across her forehead as her body tightened. John shot a glance at Stella, who was silently standing by. *How could she not understand?* thought John. Perhaps she was in denial, not looking forward to an even more rustic lifestyle. Having grown up in Seattle society, she was accustomed to creature comforts. After all, the only reason she was in Alaska was because of Thomas—being shot, rescued by Stella, and seeking his fortune in gold.

"For how long?"

"I don't know, dear. We are heavily invested in the mining claim and have to see it through."

"Can't we just go home—back to Seattle?"

John anticipated this reaction—wondering how long before Emily would actually voice it. Going back wasn't an option, especially after the disappearance of their entire fortune.

"We have little money, Emily. This is our opportunity to rebuild, to make a fresh start."

"Surely you can find the money," said Emily.

John's private investigator had little success tracing the funds. With the death of Preston Van Sant, the location was lost. Were it not for Stella, he and Emily would have been destitute—stranded in Alaska.

"I've tried. There is still a glimmer of hope, but we can't sit on our heels—we need to move forward."

"I just want to go home," said Emily, lower lip jutted out, her face taking on that all familiar look of a spoiled child. Sometimes the look worked with John, but not this time.

"You have no home," said John, pulling her aside and

leaving Stella standing alone. "You are ruining our wedding day, stop acting like a child."

Emily stood silent, looking at the floor. John grabbed her arm, squeezing hard. She snapped her head up and looked him square in the eyes. "Stop it," he said, glaring.

Stella stood back, eyes wide. This was something new—the interaction between father and daughter. Although they had spent months together, she realized she may not know either of them as well as she thought.

"Come," said Stella. "Everyone is waiting at the reception."

John's face immediately softened as he turned back to his bride. "Yes, let's get going. We don't want to keep everyone waiting," he said, taking Stella's arm in his. A final glance at Emily set her in motion, shuffling toward the door of the church.

"Cheer up, Emily," said John. "This is a day to celebrate."

† † †

The freezing water blasted him like a punch in the gut, nearly causing him to lose his breath and suck in a deep gulp. He resisted as he went under, his pack weighing him down. His feet touched bottom, the water just over his head, but the current of the river was strong—the hole in the ice threatening to fade away. Reaching over his head, Thomas pulled the short-handled axe from his trapper pack. He swung up and caught the edge of the hole, pulling his head above water. Chopping and clawing, he finally overcame the current and pulled himself halfway out. His hat gone, his hair froze instantly and he began to shake uncontrollably.

I have to get out.

Shivering, he lunged forward but slipped back toward the hole. Cracks spread in every direction, the ice threatening to give away again. In desperation, he swung the axe, gained a hold, and with what little strength remaining, pulled himself out onto the ice. Immediately his clothes began to freeze. Shaking furiously, he slipped off the pack and started to stand. The ice groaned, threatening to crack further. He laid back down and began to roll toward the bank, but his frozen glove caused him to lose grip on the pack—it rested near the open water.

Using the axe he tried to snag the strap of the pack, but it was out of reach. He crawled back toward it and his hands broke through the ice, threatening to throw him headlong into the current. Swinging at the pack again, the axe slipped from his frozen grip, skittered across the ice, and disappeared into the hole, taking the pack with it.

My matches.

Thomas rolled away from the hole, stopped flat on his back and looked up at the clear blue sky.

Have to get...off...the... The thought faded. The cold was winning, his clothes freezing, his temperature rapidly dropping.

Summoning what little strength remained, he managed to roll back to the bank and crawl up onto the shore. He tried to stand, but his muscles didn't respond. He slumped down rolling on his side. *So cold...* as he fought to stay awake. He tried to move, but it was hopeless. *Wedding day, fine day to die*, he thought. A sound in the distance—a howling—and darkness closed in.

† † †

CHAPTER 2

Applause erupted as the bride and groom entered McKinley Hall at the corner of Reservation Avenue and Hobart Street. They were all standing, turned toward the door as John and Stella entered, followed by Emily.

"Sit, please everyone," said John, shaking hands all around. "There's plenty of food and drink so enjoy."

"I'm so happy for you, Stella," said Jack as he gave her a hug. "And you too, John."

"Well thanks for standing up with me, Jack," said John. "I needed a best man and after the way you took care of the girls while I was up north you certainly owned up to the name."

Jack broke into a wide grin. "Not a problem, but I do expect you to throw more business my way."

"You can count on it. I'll have you haul everything we own to Chicken."

"Uh, forget I said anything. Not gonna make that trip with my one-horse rig," said Jack, breaking into a smile. "Say, you and Thomas are famous—have you seen the latest paper from Seattle?"

"No," said John. "How did we end up in the newspaper."

Jack leaned in closer. "Well, rumor has it that the telegraph office leaks all the interesting news—I think they must get a kickback or something."

"What did the article say?"

"It was just a little snippet among others on the gold rush up here—said you guys had a rich strike on Angel Creek."

"I hope it's rich," said John.

Jack laughed. "Well, I guess you'll find out before too—"

"Come on fellows, let's eat," said Stella.

"The bride has spoken," said Jack in a loud voice as he took his chair. "Food looks good."

John had the local eatery cater the affair with the best they could offer. It was pretty high society for the edge of the frontier. Real beef steak, potatoes, and almost-fresh vegetables brought in on the steamer from Seattle.

"May I have your attention?" said Jack standing and tapping his knife against a glass. The chatter subsided, but only after two more clangs of the knife against the glass.

Jack raised his glass. "Join me in toasting the new-lyweds, Stella and John. May you have great fortune, adventure, and love on your new journey together."

Glasses raised, the crowd heartily agreed, drinking to the new couple.

Setting his glass down, Jack surveyed the crowd. "Anyone else care to have a word?"

Noel stood up and raised his glass. "I've known Stella for a long time—John for a little while, but I believe they were made for each other. I wish them the best."

The crowd applauded with shouts of "Here, here."

"Thanks, Noel. Anyone else have a toast?" said Jack.

"I do," said a young man at the back of the room.

All eyes turned to see who was speaking, only to realize he was a stranger.

John turned to Stella and whispered, "Do you know him?"

She shook her head as he began to speak.

He stood, raised a glass, then stared directly at Stella. "It is a great honor to be here today, to witness the marriage of a woman I have longed to meet, a woman that, though she doesn't know it, has been on my mind nearly my entire life—my stepmother."

✝ ✝ ✝

Light returned slowly, dim at first, but then taking on a slowly pulsating, orange glow. Thomas opened his eyes, confused at what he saw. The last thing he remembered was laying in the snow, soaking wet and rapidly freezing. Flat on his back, he stared up at a log ceiling. The blankets weighed heavy on him, topped with what looked like a large grizzly bear rug.

"Ah, you are awake," the voice coming from somewhere in the cabin.

"Where am I?" said Thomas, struggling to raise up on his elbows.

"You are at my home," she said.

Thomas turned to look at the voice. She stood there, tall, slender, with black hair, and piercing dark eyes. Still groggy, he surveyed the modest cabin, noting the glow of the lamp and the lack of daylight outside the small window.

"How long have I been here?"

"A few hours. You have been sleeping long."

Thomas started to turn back the covers to get out of bed—only then did he realize he was completely without clothes—naked as the day he was born. He quickly dropped the covers.

"Are you cold? I can warm you again," she said.

"Warm me?" said Thomas, not sure what she meant.

"Yes, I will warm you," she said, releasing her top button.

"No!" said Thomas, pulling the covers all the way up to his neck, his face turning red. "I'm plenty warm, thank you."

She smiled at him. In another place and time, she could have been royalty—incredibly beautiful in stark contrast to the darkness outside.

"It was the only way to save you," she said. "The blankets alone would not have been enough. It is a common way."

It may have been common, but for Thomas, it was anything but. Naked in a strange cabin with a beautiful woman. *What would Emily do if she saw me now?*

† † †

CHAPTER 3

"Sit down," ordered John, jumping to his feet and pointing to the young man with the raised glass.

"But I'm not finish—"

"Sit down and shut up. You've said quite enough."

A hush fell over the crowd as the young man smiled, then slowly took his seat.

"I believe the young man has had a bit too much to drink," said Jack. "Please, let's celebrate."

An awkward pall hung over the remainder of the reception. Slowly people began to filter out, issuing their last congratulations to the happy couple. A number of folks lingered, engaged in conversation, sometimes in whispers.

John finally stood up from the table. "I want to thank you all for coming. It's meant a lot to Stella and me," he said, signaling the end of the festivities.

His face was flushed—inside he was fuming. Stella was confused and upset at what the young man had said. What should have been a joyous event took on the air of scandal.

The young man kept to himself at the back of the hall, while John, though not a violent man, was ready to rush up and grab him by the throat. *This will be the talk of the town tonight,* he thought as he made his way toward the back of the hall. Stella followed, not sure what John had in mind.

"Hello sir," said the young man, extending his hand.

John withheld his and looked him straight in the eye. "And just who in blazes are you to come in and upset things?"

The man smiled ever so slightly. By this time Stella was standing behind John, studying the young man. She was certain she had never seen him before. *What did he mean, stepmother?* Wesley had never been married before—they had known each other since their teen years.

"Name's Declan. Declan Baird."

Stella stared at him, mouth open, her hand on her chest.

"Are you looking for trouble, mister?" said John. "Because with your slander, you're asking for it."

"I may have misrepresented myself a bit, but in a way, Miss Stella is my stepmother. You see, Wesley Baird is my father."

Stella shook her head in disbelief, while John now realized he was treading unfamiliar territory, at least when it came to Stella's former husband.

"You're lying," said Stella, stepping forward forcefully. "I don't know what your game is, but I won't have you disparaging my deceased husband."

Declan took a step forward—John blocked him.

"I mean no harm. I wish you would listen to what I have to say. I have proof."

"We don't need to hear anymore," said John. "I suggest you leave, in fact, leave town before—"

"I want to hear," said Stella, gently placing her hand on John's arm.

Declan reached inside his breast pocket, pulled out a

tattered envelope, and extended his hand to Stella. She took it, removed the yellowed contents and slowly read. Exhaling deeply, her hands fell to her side as the paper floated to the floor.

Declan said nothing.

John picked it up, crumpled in his hand. "What is this?" he said, certain he saw tears welling up in Stella's eyes.

"It's a military certificate of birth," said Declan.

John unfolded the paper and read.

```
--- Certificate of Live Birth ---

Place of Birth: Fort Meade, Dakota Territory
Name of Child: Declan Baird
Date of Birth: March 25, 1879
Full Name of Father: Wesley Baird
Full Maiden Name of Mother: Melissa Harrison
```

"How can this be?" said John, turning to Stella.

Stella was staring straight ahead, not blinking.

"Stella," said John, raising his voice.

She began to cry, wringing her hands and shaking her head. "I don't know," she said through the sobs.

John had never seen her like that. She was always the strong one, never wavering under tough situations. She was completely vulnerable. He felt the heat rising up into his face.

"I didn't mean any harm," said Declan as he again tried to approach Stella.

John stepped between them, and without pause, firmly shoved Declan backward—hard.

Declan's expression immediately changed, his fists coming up as he recovered from the near fall.

John stiffened, prepared for what was to come.

"Stop," shouted Stella. "Please, just stop. I need time to think."

Declan retreated, his subtle smile returning. "Can we talk again?"

"No," said John. "You are never to come near us again."

Stella again put her hand on his arm, instantly calming him. "John, I want to go now. We will talk again young man, but not today."

"Yes, of course," said Declan. "Your wedding day and all. I'm very sorry I upset you."

Stella didn't answer as she turned John toward the door and the wagon that was waiting for them.

"Tomorrow," she said.

† † †

"Where are my clothes?" said Thomas, covers still pulled up tight around his neck.

She smiled at him, apparently finding humor in the situation. "They were frozen. I will have them dried soon."

Thomas turned his head to look around, careful not to move the covers. In the corner were his clothes, hanging from a cord strung from wall to wall near the wood stove.

"My name is Sdzeè. What is yours?"

"Uh...my name is Thomas, Thomas Thornton."

"It is very nice to meet you Thomas Thornton."

"How did I get here? Last thing I remember was crawling up the bank of the river."

"I brought you here, with help from my friends."

"Your friends?"

"My dogs. I was traveling the river with my dog team when we found you."

Thomas looked at the woman, barely over one-hundred pounds soaking wet. *Surely there is no way she could lift me into a sled.*

"I can't believe you could get me into the sled, let alone into the cabin."

"Shoh helped me."

At the sound of his name, the 120-pound dog rose from a blanket in the far corner and came trotting up to Sdzeè, tongue wagging.

"He is very strong. He helped me pull you into the cabin."

"That's an interesting name for a dog," said Thomas.

"It means bear. You can call him that if you like—he will answer to both."

"Seems appropriate," said Thomas as his head sunk back into the pillow. He was tired and realized now he hadn't eaten since morning. The smell of something delicious was floating in the air.

"What time is it?"

Sdzeè looked out the window. "It is dark."

Thomas laughed. It was dark most of the time in this part of Alaska during the winter. With less than five hours of daylight, the days were often depressingly short.

"Are you hungry? I have made a stew with udzih."

"Udzih?" said Thomas.

"Ah, you do not know the words. It is caribou."

"Well it smells delicious," said Thomas, but I really would like to get my clothes back on."

Sdzeè smiled at him, staring. Thomas began to blush.

"I think that clothes of William will fit. I will get them."

"Who is William?"

"My husband," said Sdzeè as she opened a small chest at the foot of the bed.

Thomas felt a churning in his gut. He was in for it now—naked in their bed, his imagination running wild with visions of her husband busting through the door at any moment.

"I need to get dressed and get out of here. I don't want your husband to get the wrong idea."

She looked up from the chest, a shirt and pants in her hands. Her smile faded.

"He is gone."

"I know, but he could be back at any moment."

"No, he is gone, not to come back."

"He left you here alone?"

"He died two years ago. In the mine."

Thomas felt like an idiot, especially when he saw the pain written across her face.

"I'm sorry, I didn't mean to upset you."

"It is fine. Sometimes when I remember I am sad for a moment," she said, laying the clothes on the bed. "You will dress now."

Thomas waited. Sdzeè just stood there, smiling at him from the foot of the bed. Thomas hesitated.

"Oh, you are shy. But we are good friends now."

Thomas knew what she meant, but didn't want to think about it. "Can you at least turn around while I get dressed?"

"I will go out to get wood for the stove."

Sdzeè threw on her coat and opened the door, Shoh following close behind. The blast of cold air hit Thomas in the face as the heat flowed from the cabin. "Do not be long," she said as she closed the door.

† † †

CHAPTER 4

"You will stay here with me tonight," said Sdzeè as she dropped the wood in the box next to the stove.

"I really need to be going," said Thomas, now dressed and sitting in the chair in the corner.

"It is too dark. Too cold for you to travel back to...where do you live?"

"I have a cabin on my claim at Angel Creek."

"That is too far from here. You will stay with me."

Thomas nervously eyed the only bed in the one-room cabin as he shifted in the chair made of hand-hewn birch.

Sdzeè looked at him and sensed what was going on in his mind. She smiled again.

I wish she wouldn't smile at me like that, thought Thomas.

"I will sleep in the chair," said Sdzeè. "It is big enough for me."

His gentleman instincts kicked in. "No, I can sleep in the chair."

"It is too small. You will need good rest if you are to travel home tomorrow."

Thomas relented as Sdzeè turned to the stove and began scooping up a large bowl of *udzih* stew. Fetching a spoon from the shelf above the stove, she turned and brought the steaming bowl to him. He ate ravenously, amazed at how delicious it was. The dog stared at him from the corner, apparently waiting for the empty bowl.

"You would want more?"

"Sure, if you don't mind. It's fantastic."

"I have much," said Sdzeè as she took the bowl to refill it.

His second bowl in hand, Thomas settled into the chair. Sdzeè sat on the bed, eating as well. They were quiet for a long time.

Thomas finally broke the silence. "Tell me how you came to be here."

Sdzeè smiled—there it was again—and sat her bowl on the chest at the end of the bed. "I am from Tetlin," she said as she began to relate the story of her and William. He had come into the country seeking gold like many others, and they had met, fallen in love and married. The claim was like Thomas's, frozen ground that had to be thawed then excavated. They worked the ground together for a year when the accident happened.

"William was at the bottom of the shaft when the, what are they called...cribbing gave way. It all caved in on him. I could not save him."

"I'm sorry," said Thomas.

"He is still there. At the bottom. I tried to dig but I could not get him out. He is buried with his gold."

"That is very sad, Sdzeè. I'm so, so sorry."

She looked down at the dirt floor, her hands folded in her lap. "I miss him every day. He was a good man."

Thomas looked around at the spartan accommodations. It wasn't fancy, but functional. "How do you live," he asked finally.

"I fish, hunt for grouse and caribou. In summer I pan a little gold from the creek. In winter, I trap some, but not much. I do not need much to live on."

"Have you thought of moving on? Going home?"

"I have no one left in Tetlin. I will stay here."

"Well if there is anything I can do to help you, please let me know. I owe you my life."

Sdzeè took care of her bowl, than sat down on the bed, closer to his chair now, knees almost touching. She looked straight into his eyes, smiling, saying nothing. Thomas shifted his weight in the chair, and as much as he wanted to, couldn't look away.

"You will mine for me," she said.

† † †

John paused outside the door of their hotel room. They decided to spend one night at the hotel, before returning to Stella's boarding house. It wasn't much of a honeymoon, but it was the sort of thing that was acceptable to them both.

"Should I carry you across the threshold?" said John as he swung the door open.

Stella looked up at him and laughed. "I think we're a little old for that, let's just—"

John scooped her up and carried her into the room. She blushed.

"Now put me down Mr. Palmer or there'll be trouble."

John laughed as he sat her down. The smiles lingered for a moment.

"I don't understand about Declan," said John, sobering the mood.

Stella sat down, hands shaking.

"I'm sorry, I shouldn't have brought it up," said John.

"It's fine. We need to understand."

"Why is the birth certificate from a fort in the Dakotas?"

Stella thought for a moment. "Wesley was in the army for a while after we were married. He was in the 7th Calvary assigned to Fort Meade in the Dakotas."

"When?" asked John.

"It was after the battle of Little Bighorn, I think in 1878. He was there for nearly a year. I only saw him once in that time, once when he was able to come home to Montana."

"Do you think it's possible he had another wife? Had a child with her?"

Tears came to her eyes. She and Wesley were childless—the thought of a son from another woman was almost too much. "I don't know. I can't believe he would do that to me. Yet, there is the paper—the birth certificate."

"Only you can tell if it's true. Were there any signs that made you wonder after he came back?"

"Nothing, nothing at all."

"Did he tell you about his time in the Calvary?"

"He didn't like to talk about it. What little he did say was his disgust for the senseless killing of the Sioux—women and children—it's why he got out when his time was up."

"Did he take part in that?"

"He never said, but I do know there was a lot of friction between him and the officers. I can't believe he would be a part of it."

"It seems there may be a lot we don't know about Wesley."

Stella frowned. John immediately wished he hadn't said it, realizing it was a bit insensitive.

"I'm sorry Stella."

"We need to talk to Declan."

"I'm not so sure. I think we should send him packing," said John.

"I know you don't like him, but if he is Wesley's son, we must figure out why he is here, and what he wants."

"The way he disrupted our reception is enough for me to send him on his way."

"It did put a damper on things, but let's just talk to him first," said Stella.

CHAPTER 5

Thomas woke to the smell of food drifting through the air, tickling his nose as he slowly opened his eyes. The bed was warm and for a moment he nearly forgot where he was. He sat up on one elbow, looked under the covers to make sure he was still dressed, then looked around the dimly lit cabin. It was still dark through the window and there appeared to be no one about. He threw off the covers, swung his feet over and ran his fingers through his hair, nearly down to his shoulders from the winter growth. *I should get a trim before the rest arrive from Valdez.*

He stood and confirmed that Sdzeè and the giant dog were gone. Walking over to the stove, he found last night's dinner heating—more udzih stew. He didn't mind a repeat, especially since it beat his cooking all to pieces. *Where was she?*

Just then the door opened, the icy blast surging in as Sdzeè shot through the door, firewood in her arms.

"Quick, shut the door!" she said.

Thomas complied as she dropped the wood in the box. She wasn't wearing a coat.

"You always go out without a coat in the winter?"

"No, but it was not too cold this morning. And I was only out for short minute. And it is almost spring, not winter."

Thomas laughed at her—not too cold? The tip of her nose and ears told another story.

"You will wait here, maybe stay another day," she said.

Thomas shook his head. "I have to get back. I have work to do and I've been away too long already."

"Are you sure you feel well enough to travel?"

"I'm fine. You've done too much already."

Thomas took his clothes from the drying cord and tossed them on the bed. "I need to change into my own," he said.

"You can keep what you have on. I have no use for them."

"Oh, I couldn't."

"It is fine. And your coat is like bald rabbit skin. Not warm. You need a *xaiy eek*."

Thomas looked at his wool coat. "Seems warm enough for me."

Sdzeè opened the chest and began digging through it, pushing aside shirts, a Mackinaw coat, and other items. "Ah, *xaiy eek*," she said as she lifted it from the chest.

"Oh, a parka," said Thomas.

Sdzeè shook the parka firmly and held it up. "Looks fine," she said. "Here, you try it on."

"Oh, I couldn't take it."

"No. You take it if it fits. It is very warm and has wolverine ruff. It will not freeze ice from your breath. Much better."

Thomas admired the parka. It was made from thick fur, lined, and with the heavy ruff around the hood.

"This is very nice. What kind of fur is it made from?"

"Wolf. I made it for William from ones I trapped,"

said Sdzeè.

"Really? You made this?" said Thomas, admiring the handiwork.

Sdzeè smiled at him and turned to the stove. "You hungry?"

† † †

Stella sat next to John at the corner table in the hotel restaurant. Declan sat across from them, stuffing the last mouthful of fried potatoes into his mouth. There was little conversation throughout the meal—now the breakfast of eggs, bacon, and potatoes was finished.

"Well," said John. "Tell us your story."

Declan took a gulp of coffee, wiped his mouth with the napkin and leaned back in his chair. "What do you want to know?"

"About your father, your mother, and how you came to be here," said Stella.

"Well, I don't know a whole lot really. I never met my father. My mother came down with pneumonia when I was barely a year old. She didn't make it."

"I'm sorry," said Stella. "Who raised you then?"

"I was sent to my mother's parents—my grandparents. They raised me."

"And the birth certificate?" said John.

"My grandparents gave it to me when I turned eighteen. They wanted me to have proof of who I was—in case I ever needed it."

"I still can't believe it," said Stella, shaking her head.

"I'm sorry this is upsetting to you, but I was hoping we might be a...family. I have no one. The grandparents died several years back."

John leaned back in his chair, hands clasped behind his head. He looked at the young man, shabbily dressed, looking like he had been through a rough spot. His hair was long and unkempt—his face sporting a week-old growth. "How did you find us?"

"Well, that's the interesting part. It happened quite by accident. Having no future and being of little means, I scraped my last pennies together to come north. The newspapers in all the big cities go on and on about how easy it is to get rich in Alaska, so I thought I'd give it a try—so I came to Valdez."

"How did you end up at the wedding reception?"

"Well, that's a bit embarrassing. I was looking for a free meal so I crashed the reception. I got to talking with some of the people before you arrived from the church. When I saw your last name on the reception cards I was curious. Then they told me about Wesley—Wesley Baird, and it all became clear."

"It seems it was destined to happen," said Stella.

"Quite the coincidence," said John, leaning forward.

"Look, I know you must hate me, or at the very least resent me," said Declan.

"It's not your fault. You didn't choose your parents," said Stella.

"Thank you for that."

"What are you plans now," said John.

Declan looked at Stella, then looked down at the empty plate. "Well, I'm pretty much broke. I don't have enough money for the hotel tonight, so I guess I'll have to siwash somewhere."

"Nonsense," said Stella. "You'll come back to the boarding house with us—right, John?"

John looked away, rubbing his chin. "I...uh...yes, yes.

We can't have you sleeping out on the riverbank without a tent."

"Good, it's settled," said Stella. "Get your things together and meet us out front in about thirty minutes."

"I don't know how to thank you, Miss Stella," said Declan, taking her hands in his. "You have saved me."

† † †

CHAPTER 6

Thomas finished buttoning up the parka. With all his gear somewhere at the bottom of the river, it didn't take long to get ready for the trip home.

"I guess I'm ready," he said.

Sdzeè looked him over. "You still are a Cheechako," apparently not impressed with his winter preparedness. "At least you have warm *xaiy eek* now," she said as she reached out and stroked the thick fur of the parka.

Thomas folded his arms, then took a step away. "I want to thank you for everything."

Sdzeè smiled. "You are welcome. It is good to have company. The dogs get tired of me alone."

"Well, I'll be off. I have a bit of a hike to get home," he said as he reached for the door, then paused. "Oh, I have been meaning to ask. What does your name mean?"

"It means *My heart*," said Sdzeè. "I am the first and only child of my mother and father."

Thomas smiled. "It's a beautiful name. I thank you again for all you have done. Perhaps we will meet again someday."

Sdzeè slipped past him, opened the door, then looked up into his eyes. "We will, Thomas Thornton."

† † †

Thomas reached the ridge above Angel Creek by early

29

afternoon. He paused and looked into the valley, half expecting smoke to be rising from the chimney of his cabin. It would be cold, the fire in the wood stove now only a memory. He descended the ridge, following the trail marked by a light dusting of overnight snow. All the while his thoughts turned to Sdzeè. *What did she mean "You will mine for me"? Was she serious?* She said nothing more of it—perhaps it was just her sense of humor. The image of her smiling as she said it stuck in his head.

The cabin was cold, the water he fetched the morning before now frozen in the bucket on the table. He stoked the wood stove and with a little help from some old newspaper, got a fire going. It would be a good hour or more before it warmed enough to be comfortable. He sat on the bed in the corner, thinking about the events of the last day.

I'm getting good at losing things, he thought, remembering a previous dunking in a creek and the loss of a treasured firearm. He hoped Stella had forgiven him for losing Wesley's .45-70. Though he promised to find it, the search proved fruitless, even giving it one last attempt before he and John left for Chicken. She had never mentioned it, but still, he couldn't help but wonder.

Within the hour the cabin had warmed enough for him to remove the parka—the one Sdzeè made. He admired it again as he hung it on the nail next to the door.

In a way, she reminded him of Stella—a strong, resourceful, independent woman making her way alone on the frontier. Yet, clearly she was lonely—very lonely. *I'll check up on her from time to time,* thought Thomas, the debt of gratitude owed weighing heavily on him.

After a hot cup of coffee and a bit of jerky, Thomas donned his work coat—no need to dirty the new parka—and headed to the mine shaft. Since his helper deserted him the month before, working solo on the mine slowed progress significantly. Each morning he shoveled out the thawed gravel at the face of the underground drift, hauled it to the shaft, and manually hoisted it to the surface. The "dump" of material was getting big, but not near enough to provide for an entire summer of sluicing. Once the thawed gravel was removed, he built a large fire at the end of the drift to start the overnight thaw.

It was arduous work, yet he was driven. Soon there would be four people on the mine to support. Without enough gravel to process, he wouldn't have the gold needed to provide for everyone, let alone save money to buy a boiler and hoist. Without some equipment, Thomas felt they would never make a real go of the mine. With a boiler and steam points, he could thaw the gravel without building fires underground. This, in turn, would allow them to mine in the summer, since the shaft could be covered to prevent thawing and total collapse of all the mine workings. The more he thought about it, the more heavily it weighed upon him.

He descended the shaft and made his way to the end of the drift. The temperature in the mine hovered around freezing, even when the outside was below zero, something Thomas was thankful for. Even so, with the shaft open, the cold air from the surface surged in, slowly chilling things even colder. As he expected, the fire from two days ago was long out. He swung the pick at the gravel face and it resonated like iron. The gravel had refrozen—there would be no pay dirt hauled to the surface today.

As he worked to build the fire, he thought about the wedding. *Tomorrow I need to send a telegram.*

† † †

Declan sat on the porch of Stella's boarding house, surveying the towering mountains that surrounded the Lowe River valley. He couldn't believe his good fortune—finding the wedding and Stella. He took a last sip of coffee as Stella came out the door.

"Enjoying the view?" she said.

"Yes, it's quite magnificent."

"I'm going to miss it."

"Oh?"

"Yes, we'll be heading north soon."

"Oh," said Declan. "Chicken, right?"

"Yes. It's going to be quite a change for me." Stella patted the handrail of the porch. "We'll be closing it all up for now. If we don't come back, I guess I'll put the old place up for sale. But what are your plans, young man?"

"I've been thinking about that, and...well I don't know how to ask so I just will. I'd like to come with you and help with the mine. I have no other prospects."

Stella sat on the bench beside him and stared out across the valley. Declan looked at her, waiting.

"I know you owe me nothing," he said. "But I really need this. I'm young and strong, and I wouldn't ask for much. I'll even work for free."

Stella turned and looked at him, studying his face, looking for something familiar. The color of his hair was the same, perhaps the mouth, but her memory had dimmed since that last look at Wesley years ago. Nothing in his looks or mannerisms really stood out to her. She realized she was staring and turned. "I'll talk to John."

"Talk to me about what?" said John as he came out on the porch.

Stella stood. "Declan has made a request."

"Oh?" said John looking down at him.

"He wants to come with us. To help with the mine."

The creases in John's forehead deepened as he looked at Declan. He wasn't thrilled at the prospect, especially with the way he crashed the reception. However, another person at the mine would be helpful since Thomas had lost his hired hand. The whole idea was not without complications, particularly when it came to feeding and housing one more. And besides, he wasn't sure he liked him enough to drag him along.

"Stella and I will talk about it," he said finally.

"I know I can be a real help to you. And I'd really like to get to know all of you better since I have no one else," said Declan.

"Wait here," said John as he took Stella by the arm and ushered her inside, leaving Declan alone.

"Sit," said John as he took a seat at the kitchen table. Stella sat across from him just as Emily came down the stairs.

"What's going on?" she said.

John crossed his arms and leaned back in the chair. "Declan wants to join the family."

Emily raised her eyebrows and shot a glance at Stella. "Really?"

"He has nothing else to fall back on," said Stella softly.

John snorted. "That's not really our problem."

Stella recoiled at the response—another side of John she hadn't seen before.

"Look, we don't have a lot of extra money until the mine starts paying. Can we really afford to take him on and support him? Pay him to work for us?" said John.

Emily sat down next to her father. "He might be a real help."

"So I'm the only one with doubts here? Stella?"

"Look, I know this seems like a lot all at once, but I feel like I owe him something for Wesley's sake. All he's asking is room and board—he said he would work for free."

"I need to think. And I believe we need to get Thomas's opinion," said John.

"You're right," said Stella. "We can't really spring this on Thomas unannounced."

John stood up. "I'm going to town—to send Thomas a telegram."

"I'll go with you," said Stella.

John moved towards the door. "No, I'm going alone."

† † †

"Hello? Anyone about?" said Thomas as he entered the telegraph office. It was an early spring morning in Chicken, with temperatures hovering near freezing for the first time in months. The office was empty. *Wayne probably home stoking his wood stove and drinking coffee*, thought Thomas.

The door opened behind him. "Morning," said Wayne. "You're here early."

"Had a bit of trouble the other day and failed to send an important message," said Thomas as Wayne settled into the rickety chair behind the counter.

"Another to Valdez?" said Wayne, tossing the message pad onto the counter.

Thomas scribbled on the pad, paused, pencil to his lips, then continued. "Yes. A belated congratulations."

Wayne flipped the switch and begin listening to the string of Morse code. "I closed up early yesterday. Probably in hot water with the load of messages I missed."

"What happens when you miss?"

"We're on a rotating schedule. They'll hit me again soon to see if I'm awake—ah, here they come now."

Thomas watched as Wayne responded with a few clacks of the key, then began copying the message.

"And...it's for you."

"Really? My lucky day I guess."

Wayne continued to copy, then sent a few taps on the telegraph key, tore the sheet off the pad and handed it to Thomas. "Maybe not."

Thomas frowned. It was wonderful to be able to communicate with the outside world, but he didn't appreciate the fact his business wasn't private. *How many people between here and there—*"

"Your message ready?"

"Not quite," said Thomas as he began to read.

```
THOMAS THORNTON / CHICKEN ALASKA

ODD DEVELOPMENT HERE. COMPLICATED.
TOO MUCH TO EXPLAIN.

ARE YOU OPPOSED TO HOUSING ONE
MORE? WESLEY'S SON WANTS TO WORK
FOR ROOM AND BOARD.

I HAVE DOUBTS.

JOHN PALMER / VALDEZ ALASKA
```

Wesley's son? thought Thomas. *What in the world is this about?* Questions flooded his mind, but it seemed pointless to request more information. Having three more people on the claim was one thing—adding another unknown was troubling, yet there was no doubt they could use the help, especially if they didn't have to pay wages. Then there was the fact that John appeared to have doubts. Thomas completed the congratulatory message to Stella and John, then penned another to John alone:

```
JOHN PALMER / VALDEZ ALASKA

REGARDING WESLEY'S SON, I LEAVE
IT UP TO YOUR JUDGMENT, NOT
KNOWING FULL SITUATION.

WE CERTAINLY COULD USE THE HELP.

THOMAS THORNTON / CHICKEN ALASKA
```

Thomas handed both messages to Wayne. "Put the charge on my account and send those immediately."

"Aye Aye captain," said Wayne, giving an animated salute.

Thomas left without saying goodbye.

Wonder what that's all about? thought Wayne as he pondered the two messages. He settled back into the chair and began tapping on the key. *Seems like there may be trouble brewing on Angel Creek.*

† † †

CHAPTER 7

John Palmer was at the Valdez telegraph office early, hoping for a reply from yesterday's message to Thomas. He almost hoped Thomas would nix the whole idea, giving him an easy out with Stella. He swore under his breath. *Just married and this has to crop up.*

"Excuse me Mr. Palmer?" said the clerk. "Did you say something?"

"Oh, no. Just thinking out loud. Do you have anything for me?"

The clerk shuffled through a small stack of messages. John realized it was a long-shot. Odds that Thomas got his message so quickly were slim.

"You're in luck. Got one from up north. No, wait—two," said the clerk, handing the messages to John.

John read the congratulatory message, pocketed it, then read the next. *Great, it all rests on me.*

On the ride back to the boarding house, John weighed his options, only to realize there was only one. It was clear what Stella wanted, and Emily certainly wasn't opposed. As he approached the house, it became obvious—despite his doubts, Declan would go north with them.

The horse snorted as John rounded the last bend. The house came into view, and he saw Emily sitting on the porch, smiling and engaged in what appeared to be lively conversation. And then there was Declan—sitting next to her with his chair pulled close, leaning in, his hands nearly touching hers.

John frowned. "Shouldn't you be packing?" he shouted, a growl in his voice.

Declan looked his way, smiled, and didn't move.

† † †

Thomas hoisted the last of the thawed gravel to the surface. It took the better part of the day to complete the task. He hurried to fetch the wood needed to build the fire at the face of the workings, but his thoughts were on the latest development in Valdez. Realizing he should have requested an immediate reply from Palmer, he now felt a bit in limbo. The lack of housing for three or four more people weighed heavily on him.

With the fire burning, he gathered up the pick and shovel and began the retreat to the shaft.

"Hello? Are you down there?"

At first, he thought he was hearing things, but the voice came again.

"Thomas Thornton, are you there?" the voice came faintly again.

"Who is it?" he yelled but heard nothing more.

He hurried and reached the shaft. Looking up, he saw Sdzeè's smiling face looking down.

Thomas stacked the tools against the shaft wall and stepped on the ladder. "I'll be right up."

Sdzeè grabbed his hand as he reached the top rung of the ladder and hoisted him out, Thomas struggling to keep up.

"Thanks," said Thomas, blushing slightly.

"You are welcome. I have come to talk business."

Thomas slapped his hands against his pants, trying in vain to remove the dirt. "Business?"

"Yes. I am ready for you to mine for me."

Thomas grabbed his chin. "I thought you were joking about that."

"No. Why would you think that?"

"I..."

Sdzeè crossed her arms, staring at him. "Well?"

Thomas didn't make eye contact. "Help me cover the shaft, then we'll go up to the cabin and talk."

Sdzeè obliged, the smile never leaving her face.

"You want coffee?" said Thomas as he stoked the wood stove.

Sdzeè sat at the table, hands crossed, studying his every move. "Yes."

Thomas clanked the pot down on the stove to heat the remains of the morning brew. In only a few minutes there were two steaming tin cups of coffee on the table.

Sdzeè clasped her hands gently around the cup and looked across the table, waiting.

Thomas looked across at her, the silence becoming unbearable as he searched for words. "Look, I'm eternally grateful to you, but I am really in a bind here. I'm working the claim here alone and I have three or four people coming soon with no place to house them. I don't see how I can drop everything and work your mine."

"Four?"

"Yes, my partner and his wife and daughter, and maybe another fellow I've not met."

She put the cup down and slid it away from her. "I see."

"You're upset."

There was no hint of that haunting smile on her face. "You said if there was anything you could do to help me—now you forget?"

Thomas remembered saying it.

"Are you a man of your word, Thomas Thornton?"

It stabbed at his heart. As if there wasn't enough stress, now his integrity was being challenged. Sdzeè reached across the table and placed her hands on his, staring intently into his eyes. The temptation to look away was great, but he withstood her gaze, keeping his hands in place.

"Yes, I am."

† † †

Stella looked around the boarding house, wondering how much of her life she dare take north. There were so many things and so many memories in every nook and cranny, she worried about closing up the house and leaving it. They were limited to one trunk each on the wagon line, leaving little room for extras. Anything else needed on the claim would have to be shipped separately at great cost. Stella resigned herself to taking only the essentials.

"Packed?" said John as he came down the stairs.

"Not completely," said Stella. "It's hard to leave so much behind. I worry about it. Perhaps we should have hired a caretaker or someone to keep the house open."

"We are a bit tight on funds, especially with the passage north. I think it will be alright. I've asked Jack to keep an eye on the place as he goes by now and then." John hesitated. "We could have sold it."

The words stung a bit. Selling amounted to eliminating the last vestiges of her life with Wesley. Guilt spread over her, almost as though she was unfaithful to her new husband. Yet it was so much to let go of—a hard-fought life on the frontier.

"I'm not ready to sell," she said flatly.

"I know. Sorry for mentioning it."

Stella brushed by him and started up the stairs. "Don't worry about it. I need to finish packing my things. By the way, have you seen the pocket watch I keep on the bureau?"

"You mean Wesley's?"

"You know?"

"Thomas told me about finding it."

It was a day she would never forget—the day Thomas returned from the mountains with the watch and the news of finding Wesley. It was a bittersweet day and the watch was the last remaining testament.

"Haven't seen it," said John. "I'll keep an eye out. I'm sure we'll find it."

Stella sighed. *Where could it be?*

Emily bounded down the stairs, nearly slamming into Stella. "Oh, sorry. Father, can I take two trunks? One is simply not enough."

"Of course, dear. If you want to walk and drag the other behind you."

"I think this trip is making everyone crabby," said Emily as she plopped down on a chair. "I need my things."

"Sorry. One trunk each."

"But Declan has nothing. There should be room since he's not taking a trunk."

John sighed. "You aren't going to need all those things on the mining claim."

"But what if I want to go to town."

John laughed.

"Why do you laugh?"

"You'll understand when you see the town. Believe me, you aren't going to need all those fancy dresses you want to take."

Emily frowned. "This doesn't sound like any fun at all. What am I going to do all day?"

"Probably shovel gravel, wash dishes, butcher caribou, and chop wood."

Emily's mouth dropped.

"All that while living in a tent," said John.

Emily sighed as her lower lip jutted out.

"Just kidding," said John. "At least about some of it."

Emily stood, and placed her hands firmly on her hips. "You're not funny," she said as she turned and stormed off, pushing past Stella once again.

"Finish packing," yelled John as the door slammed upstairs.

Stella walked slowly down the stairs. "You're not making this any easier for her."

"I know. Just trying to have a little fun, but it turned into another drama," said John. "We need to get things in order—the stage leaves in three days."

"I'll be packed by the end of the day, except for those last-minute things I need."

"That gives us a couple of days to finish closing up things around here," said John, looking out the window. "If we can get that boy to help at all."

Declan sat on the porch, his feet up, smoking a cigarette and gazing out at the mountains that towered above the Lowe River. He spent most of his time "relaxing" as he put it. John wasn't sure why he needed to relax—he hadn't witnessed him do a single thing other than take up space, talk incessantly with Emily, and eat their food. If this was any indication of his character, he certainly wasn't going to be a help on the claim but a burden.

"I sure hope it's not a mistake—taking him with us."

Stella came up behind and put her hand on his shoulder. "I know you're not thrilled, but you know my reasons. I'll talk to him."

"Probably better you than me, but if he doesn't pull his weight, I'm ditching him first chance."

"I'm sure he has good intentions. Maybe he's just a little lost with no direction."

"He's going to be a lot lost if he doesn't prove up."

"Oh John. You play a tough guy at times, but I know you're all heart."

John huffed, then smiled. "If you say so. I"m going to go see if I can't light a fire under Emily."

Stella laughed and shook her head, then turned and went out on the porch.

† † †

Thomas stared down into the collapsed hole, now a slumped pit of muck and broken timbers. The afternoon was warm, remarkably so compared to the week before. It was clear spring was coming. Everywhere the sun touched, the snow and ice retreated. The open hole and mud had thawed, at least a few inches on the surface. Thomas shook his head, rubbed his chin, and turned to look at Sdzeè.

"So he's still down there?"

"William? Yes. I told you I could not save him."

Thomas wasn't real thrilled at the prospect of digging up a body. After a bit of negotiation, he had agreed to open up the mine for her to get access to the drifts.

She had pressed him to work full time for her but finally agreed to scale back her requests. As it was, it still amounted to a huge job—one that would divert Thomas from his tasks—tasks that *had* to be done before the rest of them arrived from Valdez. *Good thing the days are getting longer,* he thought. *I'm going to be working eighteen hours a day.*

"Can you do it?"

Thomas stared back down the hole. "How deep was it to the bottom?"

"I am not sure. Maybe twenty feet...or could be thirty."

Twenty feet or more of frozen muck, gravel, and timber to work through was overwhelming. This shaft was in the same condition as the one on his claim used to be—with the added complication of a body.

"Might be easier to dig a new shaft," said Thomas.

"But this one is already here."

"I know, but see how it's caved in and is wider at the top. It will continue to cave in as we dig it out so we'll have to timber it as we go and still have problems."

The trick was to sink a new shaft so it intersected the workings at the bottom. Thomas realized if he missed, it would be difficult to figure out which direction to go along bedrock to find the existing drifts.

"Do you know which direction the workings go from the bottom of the shaft?"

Sdzeè stared at the shaft, then pointed upstream along the creek. "I think it goes that way."

"Are you sure?"

Sdzeè held her chin and looked downstream. "Yes, I am sure. Upstream."

"And how long is the drift in that direction?"

"I am not sure, but it must be near forty feet."

"That's a start," said Thomas. At least he knew where to site the shaft and which way to drift.

"What is your plan Thomas Thornton?"

He wondered why she used his full name most of the time. It reminded him of when he was young. Hearing his full name from his mother meant he was in trouble. Now it was just her way.

"I think the best thing to do is move upstream at least twenty or thirty feet, and away from the creek perhaps fifteen feet, then sink the new shaft. Once we get down far enough, we can drift perpendicular to the creek and intersect the workings."

It was a feasible plan, but a lot of work—more than he could really manage.

"Shall we start?" said Sdzeè

Thomas started to frown but hid it. "Now?"

"Yes."

Thomas looked around at the melting snow, still too deep to reveal the ground in many places. A pain jabbed at his stomach. *This it too much, what with Stella and all arriving before long.*

"I can't really get started until after my partner and family arrive. I have to get things ready for them to arrive."

"You have family?"

"Well...sort of. You know, I already mentioned them—my fiancée, her father, and new wife."

Sdzeè stared at him. Thomas shuffled his feet, then turned from her gaze.

"Fiancée? You did not say fiancée before."

"Yes, her name is Emily."

"I see. So it is not real family—yet. And when are you to be married?"

Thomas turned and started back toward the cabin, then paused. "As soon as I've made my fortune."

Sdzeè followed, then touched his shoulder. Thomas stopped and turned.

"I will help. We are partners now. Fifty-fifty on the mine, and I will come help prepare for your friends to come."

"You don't have to do that—it's too much. I haven't done anything to gain that kind of interest in your mine."

"You will," she said, a smile spreading across her face. "You will."

CHAPTER 8

Thomas poured a cup of coffee and slumped into the chair. The last ten days were brutal—keeping up with the thawing in the mine while trying to get housing ready for the group. Sdzeè helped with it all, and as they worked together, Thomas became more impressed with the self-reliant young woman.

"More firewood," said Sdzeè as she came bursting through the cabin door, arms full of wood. She dropped it next to the stove, then sat down across from Thomas.

"You need to take a break," said Thomas. "You've been on the go for the last ten days."

"You too. But you are tired and I am not," she said, breaking into a wide grin.

"Well, we're about done. Just need to finish up a few little things. I hope it's all good enough."

After John's latest telegram stating four of them would be coming, Thomas opted to construct a wood platform, set on a temporary log foundation to serve as the floor for the large canvas tent that was to be the men's dorm. With some cots and a small table, along with the barrel stove Thomas fashioned, it would have to work. It wasn't ideal, keeping the newlyweds apart, but that would have to wait until the thaw when proper accommodations could be constructed. It was still too early in the spring to think about building a house.

"When do they arrive?" said Sdzeè.

"I expect this afternoon or tomorrow according to the stage schedule—assuming they didn't have any trouble along the way."

"Shall we go to town and see?"

Thomas looked down and shuffled in his seat. He liked her. Was it because she saved his life or...?

Sdzeè slammed her palm on the table. "You sleeping with your eyes open?"

Thomas jumped, nearly falling over backwards. This brought a roaring laugh from Sdzeè.

"Well?" she said, looking him squarely in the eye.

"I guess I should, but you don't have to go with me. You probably want to be getting home."

Sdzeè rocked back in her chair, arms folded. "You don't want me to go?"

Thomas was torn. He didn't want to hurt her feelings, but now that Emily drew near, her presence might complicate things—might lead to an uncomfortable misunderstanding. He certainly was worried about the tale of his rescue being told—well at least the part that took place in Sdzeè's cabin.

"No, it's not that," he stammered.

"What is it then?"

Thomas didn't have an answer—at least not a convenient one. He quickly gulped the last of his cold coffee, then stood. "Come on, let's go."

Sdzeè jumped up, leaped around the table, then gently nudged him on the shoulder, her hand remaining for a moment. Without saying anything, she smiled, then bolted for the door. Thomas stood frozen in place.

"Come on, don't just stand there!" she said as she swung the door open. "They might be there already!"

† † †

Emily slogged through the mud to the stage, trying to hold her dress clear, but finding it pointless. The damp wicked up her dress, soaking it halfway to her knee with a nice brown color.

"Look at this!" she said, pointing at the mess, then grabbing her father's hand as he helped her up into the seat. "I am so sick of this trip."

The open stage had little in the way of comfort, leaving one exposed entirely to the elements.

"It won't be long now, dear," said John, trying in vain to ease her irritation. "This is the last rest stop before Chicken."

Emily tugged to straighten her muddy dress. "Some rest stop."

"Cheer up Emily. Soon you'll see Thomas," said Stella.

"Well I for one am ready to be done with the trip as well," said Declan, as he slowly swept his hands across Emily's shoulders from the seat behind. His hands lingered.

She turned, but didn't say anything, relieved that her father hadn't witnessed the event.

"How long before we get there?" said Emily, her tone moderating.

The driver whipped the reins, the horses straining against the mud, then finally moving forward. The stage churned on through the muddy ruts. "Oh, I expect we'll be there by mid-afternoon," said the driver, not looking her way.

"Good," said Emily. "I can't wait to get a hot bath and put on my good dress."

The driver chuckled, then spit tobacco out the side of

his mouth. "Good luck with that, missy," he said, whipping the reins hard.

Emily huffed. "What do you mean good—"

John gave her a look that stopped her mid-sentence. "Just relax Emily. We'll be there before long and once you get to the claim, I'm sure you'll appreciate our new home."

Emily shook her head. "What have you gotten us into, Father?"

"I'm sure it will be fine," said Stella. "The important thing is we'll all be together."

Emily frowned and stared off into the distance, hoping the mud flinging off the wheels would stay away.

"She'll be fine once we get there," said Stella, whispering closely into John's ear.

He wasn't so sure. Stella would be fine—she'd roughed it before. Emily, on the other hand, fancied herself a bit of a princess. John purposely didn't give her too many details on what lie ahead.

"I hope so," he said. "Otherwise it's going to be a long summer."

† † †

Thomas looked out the cafe window again, his left leg bouncing up and down uncontrollably. Sdzeè took another sip from her coffee, sat the cup down, and slapped the table—hard. Thomas jumped, spilling his cup in the process.

"Would you stop that!" he said. "What is it with you and slapping tables?"

"You nervous, Thomas Thornton?"

"No. Why?"

"Oh, I don't know. Maybe because your leg has been hopping like a snowshoe hare with a lynx nipping at its heels."

Thomas frowned. "Nice. I'm not nervous."

Sdzeè stared into his eyes, then laughed. "Sure. I believe you."

Thomas, sopped up the mess with his handkerchief, all the while wondering how he let himself get into such an awkward situation. He just hoped Sdzeè wouldn't make it even more awkward.

"I hope they get here soon," said Sdzeè as she peered out the window.

Thomas wasn't sure why she was so excited about the arrival. "Maybe they were delayed," he said, secretly hoping it was true—delayed until maybe Sdzeè wasn't around.

Sdzeè stood and looked out the window. "You want another cup of coffee? I will get it for you."

"No thanks. I don't want to spill another one when you have your next slapping spell."

She glared at him—then laughed out loud. "You are so funny, Thomas Thornton."

"I'm glad you think so," said Thomas as the sound of a horse snorting reached his ears.

"Sounds like the stage is here," shouted Sdzeè as she headed for the door.

"Wait!" said Thomas. "Let me go first."

Sdzeè paused, then stepped aside, a big smile on her face as she opened the door. "Be my guest."

Thomas stumbled out the door, nearly falling face-first into the mix of snow and mud on the street. Gaining his balance, he turned and saw not a stage, but a single horse slogging down the street, carrying a ragged miner from one of the nearby creeks.

"False alarm," said Sdzeè. "Looks like we have time for more coffee."

Thomas trudged back into the building and plopped down at the table. *More waiting.* "Maybe you should head home, Sdzeè. No need for you to hang around if it's going to be late."

"No, I will stay. I wouldn't miss this for anything," she said.

Thomas felt a slight stab in his gut, his hope of avoiding an awkward situation fading.

Another hour passed, then two—still nothing. Thomas began to worry that something had gone wrong on the trail.

Sdzeè jabbed him in the shoulder. "Stop looking so worried, Thomas Thornton. They will be here soon. The trail can be slow this time of year."

"I'm not worried," said Thomas, telling a half-truth. He was worried, more so about Sdzeè being there than the stage being late. "You sure you don't want to head home? I hate to make you sit here all day."

Sdzeè smiled. "I have nothing else to do today."

† † †

The wagon shifted violently to the left as the front wheel came apart, throwing Emily into the mud and slush. John flailed desperately, his attempt at grabbing her failing.

"Emily! Are you okay?"

Emily rolled over into a sitting position, sobbing loudly as the mud slithered from her dress. Declan hopped off the wagon.

"Here let me help you up," he said, extending his hand.

Emily shifted from sobbing to wailing, not looking up, apparently unable to hear Declan over her own cater-wauling. Declan grabbed her hand just as John reached her.

"Let's get her up," he said.

They lifted her from the mud, her lower lip quivering in between howls.

"Emily. Get a hold of yourself. Are you hurt?" asked John.

"My dress is ruined," she said, flinging her arms to her side, mud flying in all directions.

"Don't worry about the dress. Are you hurt?"

Her tears turned to a scowl. "No, Father. I'm not hurt, but I am sick of this trip."

"We need to get you into some dry clothes. Stella, can you fetch something from her trunk?"

Stella moved to the back of the wagon to find Emily's trunk.

"I'm not getting undressed out here. There's no place to change."

"Got a spruce tree over yonder," said the driver as he surveyed the broken wheel.

"I'm soaked to the bone. If you think I'm stripping down out here you have another thing coming."

"Ride wet then. I don't care," said the driver.

John shot him a narrow glance the driver immediately understood.

"I best see to this wheel," he said.

"Good idea," said John.

Stella pulled a fresh set of clothes and undergarments

from the trunk, along with a sheet. "Here Emily, let's get off the trail and over behind that tree. I'll hold a sheet up while you change."

"This is ridiculous," she said, reluctantly slogging off the trail toward the tree.

John turned his attention to the wagon. "What's the damage?"

The driver rubbed his chin and stared at the wheel, now a miscellaneous assortment of wood and iron. "Not good."

An understatement, thought John. "I can see that. Can we fix it?"

"We have a spare wheel onboard, the problem is we seem to have lost the axle bolt."

"Axle bolt?"

"Some wagons use a big nut, but this axle uses a long bolt to hold the wheel on. Looks like it wasn't tight and worked its way out. That's why we lost the wheel."

John started looking around, sweeping his wet boots through the soupy mud.

"It's going to be hard to find. Could'a come out a mile back for all we know."

"Wouldn't the wheel fall off before that?"

"Not necessarily. Might'a rode on the spindle for a while."

"Well, we better start looking for it," said John. "Why don't you carry a spare bolt?"

The driver spit, the chew hitting the mud with a splat. "Never needed one."

John looked back down the trail. It was a sea of mud and water, sometimes half a foot deep. Finding the bolt would be near impossible without crawling on hands and knees sweeping through the slop.

"What shall we do?" asked John.

"You and your boy work on getting the wagon raised up so we can get the new wheel on. Me and the ladies will look for the bolt."

Declan bristled at the word boy. "I'm nobody's boy."

"Sorry, sonny, ain't got time for proper salutations. If we don't get this fixed, we'll be spending the night here."

Declan glared at the driver, his fist slowly closing. As he started forward, he saw John staring at him. His fist relaxed and the glare changed to a tight smile. "Let's get it done."

Emily returned from her changing. "Did I hear someone say spend the night? This just keeps getting better and better."

"You've got a job to do," said John. "Help Stella look for the axle bolt while we get the new wheel on."

"Bolt?"

The driver grabbed her hand and nearly drug her to the rear wheel. "That's what we're looking for," he said, pointing to the bolt. "It's about six inches long with threads on it."

Emily ripped her hand away and smoothed her dress. Stella put her hand on Emily's shoulder. "Come, let's see if we can find it. Where should we look?"

"I'll claw through the mud where the wheel came off." The driver pointed back down the trail. "You two walk the trail back and see if you can spot it."

"Come on Emily," said Stella. "Let's find it."

As they walked back down the trail, nearly losing their balance as they slipped into the deep ruts, the mud slowly seeped up the hem of Emily's clean dress.

† † †

"Staring at it isn't going to make time go faster, Thomas Thornton," said Sdzeè.

Thomas put away the pocket watch as the fading light of day filtered through the window. "Something must have happened—be pitch dark in another hour."

Sdzeè waved at the proprietor. "Bring us some of your caribou stew, please. And biscuits."

Thomas sat silent. The man returned with the food and set it on the table. Sdzeè nodded at him and smiled.

"I'm not really hungry," said Thomas.

"Sure you are. You just do not know it," she said. "Eat and if they are not here when we finish, I think we should go."

Thomas knew she was right. It wasn't likely the stage would show up after dark. Traveling the trail was hazardous enough at times, and crossing the narrow bridge across the Mosquito Fork in the dark was not a wise action. As it was, it would be nearly dark when they headed back to the claim.

Dinner over, Thomas wondered how long he should wait. Sdzeè knew what he was thinking.

"They are not coming today," she said. "Already it is too dark. We should go."

Thomas now faced another small, or perhaps big, dilemma. It was too late in the day for Sdzeè to travel all the way back to her cabin. Reluctantly, he decided.

"Why don't you stay at the claim tonight? It's too late and too far for you to get home safely."

"Thank you, Thomas Thornton. I will."

"You can have the cabin, I'll try out the new men's dormitory. And please, call me Thomas from now on."

Sdzeè smiled, then stood. "Okay, Thomas. Come, let us go home."

† † †

CHAPTER 9

It was a cold night, huddled in the modest canvas tent with no heat. The search for the axle bolt was fruitless, despite everyone looking until dark. The stage carried little in the way of camping gear since all overnight stops were supposed to be at a roadhouse. Everyone had sorted through their belongings, pulling out anything that would serve to keep them warm. Morning came with a cold drizzle falling, intermixed with the occasional snow flake.

Emily emerged from the tent, the last to exit. The others were standing around a small campfire John built, waiting for a pot of coffee to boil. Though the stage carried limited supplies, everyone was thankful coffee was on board.

"Well this is just a lovely morning," she said. She stared at the driver. "Why aren't you fixing the wagon?"

He snorted and turned away.

"Well?" she demanded.

"Emily, hush," said her father.

"I just want to know what he is going to—"

"I said be quiet. Hold your tongue. You're not helping."

Emily huffed and turned her back to them. Stella started towards her but changed her mind.

"How far are we from Chicken?" said John.

The driver rubbed his chin and looked down the trail. "Probably ten, maybe fifteen miles."

"A long walk," said John.

"I'm not walking," said Emily. "I—"

John glared at her and she stopped. He turned to the driver. "What do you suggest?"

"Well, the horses aren't keen on being ridden, but this one here has had some saddle time. Don't have a saddle—I'll have to ride her bareback into town and scrounge up a bolt somewhere."

"How long will it take?"

"Not sure. I should be able to get back in time and fix the wheel so we can get underway and make it to town before dark."

"What are we supposed to do all day?" said Emily.

"Sit in the tent and complain I suppose," said the driver, his eyes narrowing. "I'm going to get the horse ready, have a swig of coffee, and get going. You folks make sure everything is packed up so we can get moving as soon as possible when I return."

John nodded, hoping the rain would stop. It was going to be a long day, particularly with one of the party's sour mood.

Coffee done, horse readied, the driver mounted up and nudged the horse forward, hoping he could hold on without the benefit of a saddle.

"Good luck," said John, waving him on.

"Thanks. I'll bring something to eat back with me," he said as the horse plodded down the trail.

They watched until he finally disappeared around a bend, then looked at each other. No one spoke for a while.

"Now what?" said Declan, finally breaking the silence.

"We wait," said John.

"I'm hungry," said Emily. "Is there nothing to eat?"

"There's a bit of hardtack here if you want some," said Stella, extending her hand.

Emily turned up her nose. "Disgusting."

Stella looked at her, pausing with her hand outstretched. *How is this girl going to make it?* For an instant she considered giving her a talking to, but decided it would likely fall on deaf ears—at least today.

Declan snatched the hardtack from Stella's hand and bit down hard, pieces crumbling and falling from the corner of this mouth. "Delicious," he said, then feigned a grin.

"You're going to get hungry before the day is out," said John.

"Maybe, but I'm not eating a dried up shingle pretending to be bread," said Emily.

"Suit yourself," said John.

† † †

Thomas rolled over a bit too far and fell out of the cot onto the rough wood floor. The night wasn't pleasant—the dormitory tent was a bit breezy and the wood stove was long out, making for a cold night. He picked himself up off the floor and sat on the edge of the cot. When he and John first arrived at the claim, Thomas thought the cabin was pretty rough. Now it seemed the epitome of comfort.

Thomas pulled on his pants and buttoned his shirt. *Something has happened.* Worry began to set in, but he shook it off. The trail could be slow going this time of year. Surely they must be fine. He stuffed his arms into his coat and left the tent. *I hope Stella is okay.*

Reaching the cabin, Thomas pulled open the door to find Sdzeè standing at the stove, back to him, dressed only in a long flannel shirt that went to just above the knee. She was standing on the dirt floor, barefoot.

"Oh," said Thomas, turning. "Sorry, I should have knocked."

Sdzeè turned, steaming cup of coffee in hand. "Do not be ridiculous. Sit down. Coffee is ready."

"Uh...I'll go back to the tent until you're decent."

Sdzeè laughed. "You think I am not decent?"

"That's...not what I meant. Just you aren't dressed."

"You are silly. I am nearly so—it is my shirt," she said. "It is no different than wearing a dress."

A short one. Thomas supposed she was correct, yet he felt his face burning hot. He backed up and pulled the door open. "I'll be back in a minute."

Stupid, he thought as he heard Sdzeè giggling on the other side of the door. *Should've known better than to just walk in.*

He started for the dorm tent, then paused, looked back at the cabin, unsure what to do, then continued on. The cabin door opened with a creaking sound loud enough to be heard down at the creek.

"You can come back now," said Sdzeè.

Thomas stopped, not turning. He didn't know why she made him uncomfortable, but deep down he had a suspicion.

"Come on," she yelled. "Coffee is getting cold."

Thomas turned, relieved to see a fully dressed Sdzeè, and made his way into the cabin and pulled a chair up to the table.

Sdzeè handed him a cup of coffee and sat down, smiling as usual. "Are you ready for today?"

"What do you mean?" said Thomas.

"Are you ready to see Emily? I know I can not wait to meet her—this woman who has captured your heart."

Thomas blushed.

Sdzeè's face broke into a wide smile. "What is wrong?" she said, with a playful tone.

Thomas shrugged. "Nothing."

"You do not hide your feelings well. You are nervous."

She was right. Of course he was nervous about a lot of things, but mostly how Emily would react when he shows up with a young woman in tow. *This could be messy*, he thought, knowing full well he had nothing to feel guilty about. Without Sdzeè he would have been dead—a frozen lump on a forgotten river bank. Without her, the arrival preparations wouldn't have been completed. She was a friend—a good and loyal friend. *I dare not hurt her.*

"Look Sdzeè, you really don't have to go with me. I'm sure you must have things that need attending at your place."

"Are you trying to get rid of me, Thomas Thornton?"

"Well...uh, no. I just feel bad that you have spent so much of your time helping," said Thomas, hoping the lie—no—untruth would fly.

"I will return home once your people arrive."

It was the best he could hope for, though not ideal. He was pretty sure of Emily's reaction, but not so sure about John and Stella. *It's all completely innocent* he thought, hoping others would see it the same way.

Sdzeè slammed her fist on the table jolting Thomas.

"Stop daydreaming again. We must go soon, should we not?"

Thomas shook his head. "Will you ever stop doing that?"

Sdzeè just smiled and took another sip of her coffee.

"I don't relish spending the whole day in town waiting, but I guess there is no other option. It would be bad to miss their arrival."

"Exactly," said Sdzeè.

† † †

The day wore on, yet still no sign of the driver. Emily became increasingly annoying, complaining about everything imaginable. Declan was constantly at her side, agreeing with her every word.

"When will we get out of this god-forsaken place?" said Emily, stomping her foot, voice shrill.

"I would never have let this happen, especially to you," said Declan.

"As if you could prevent it," said John, staring at him intently.

Declan stepped towards him, eyes narrowed, then stopped and smiled. "One could try," he said.

"Patience everyone," said Stella. "I'm sure he will return soon."

Emily huffed, turned her back, and walked away, Declan trailing behind her.

"I don't think I trust him," said John with a whisper.

"I too am beginning to have my doubts," said Stella as she watched the two walk down the muddy trail.

"I plan to keep a close eye on him," said John.

An hour passed, then the sound of hoof beats reached their ears. The driver rounded the corner, now bouncing up and down in a borrowed saddle, the horse sporting mud up to its flanks. He pulled the reins up short and slowly climbed down.

"You made it," said John.

"Finally. Took a while to find a bolt—had to steal, er...borrow one from another wagon. Then took me another hour to find a saddle I could borrow. Didn't want to make that trip bareback a second time."

"Was there anyone waiting for us in town?" said Emily.

The driver looked at her, standing there, arms crossed, staring at him. "Didn't ask."

"He's a young man, Thomas Thornton."

"Don't know the name, but I did see a young fellow at the roadhouse sitting with an Indian woman."

"That can't be him," said Emily.

"Sorry, can't help you," he said, pulling the axle bolt from the horse's pack. "Let's get this thing fixed and get underway. Three hours and we can be in Chicken."

† † †

Thomas drummed his fingers on the table and stared out the window. He and Sdzeè had been at the roadhouse now for a couple of hours. The proprietor approached carrying two more cups of coffee.

"I'm going to have to start charging you rent," he said as he set the cups down.

"Sorry," said Thomas.

"No problem I guess—as long as you keep buying coffee, and maybe a meal or two."

The door swung open and the owner of the sawmill looked around, then walked up to the counter.

"Coffee?" said the proprietor.

"If you got nothing stronger," he said, then smiled.

The proprietor poured him a cup of mud and set it on the counter. "What's new?"

"Not much. Guess the Valdez stage is broke down up in the hills about ten, fifteen miles out."

Thomas immediately perked up.

"What happened?" said the proprietor.

"Guess they lost a wheel. The driver was here this morning and borrowed an axle bolt. Rode in bareback and was looking for a saddle last I saw him."

"I thought that was him but wasn't sure. He grabbed some coffee and gulped it. Looked like he was in a hurry," said the proprietor.

Thomas stood up. "Did he say anything about the passengers?"

"Nothing particular. Just that he needed to get the wagon fixed and get them into town."

"How long ago?" said Thomas.

"Been a while. Didn't you see the fellow come in?" said the proprietor.

"No, I wasn't paying attention. Did he say anything to you?"

"Nope."

The sawmill owner laughed. "The stage doesn't like to advertise their misfortunes. Might hurt business, even though they don't have much competition. Small town though—word will get around."

"I should head up there," said Thomas. "Make sure everything is alright."

"Kinda pointless. He's probably back and got her fixed by now."

Sdzeè shook her head in agreement. "They will be here soon, Thomas, probably before you could get ready.

If they don't come in a few hours, we will go help them."

Thomas sat down, now more anxious than ever, fighting the urge to do something.

"Relax, you are making me nervous," said Sdzeè with a wink. "I am sure everything is good."

† † †

"Almost there," said the driver as the wagon crossed the crude log bridge over the Mosquito Fork.

"Yep, I remember this part of the trip well. Couldn't wait to get to Chicken," said John.

The trail followed the base of the hills, winding along with a slow descent into town. All in the wagon were anxious, especially after the long delay. Rounding the last bend, the town came into view.

"That's it?" said Emily. "Where's the rest of it?"

The driver laughed, continually amazed at her complaining. "It's a frontier town missy—ain't no Seattle."

Emily huffed and crossed her arms while the rest took in the view.

"Certainly different from Valdez," said Stella. "But I remember the day when it looked just like this."

"It's going to be a different lifestyle, but will pay off big in the long run," said John. "We've got a good claim and with a little luck, we'll be set for life."

"I hope so," said Declan, taking a long drag on his cigarette.

John looked at Stella, then at Declan who had a thin smile on his face. *Surely he doesn't think he has an equal stake,* thought John, unsure of where Stella was coming from. *Something to sort out later.*

They passed a number of small log cabins and several tiny, wood-frame houses that lined the muddy main street of Chicken, finally pulling up in front of the livery next to the roadhouse.

"This is it said the driver. Unload your stuff now—I'm already a day and a half late to Eagle."

Emily remained perched on the seat, looking around. "I thought Thomas would meet us."

"Get down missy, I got things to do," said the driver.

Declan was already down, watching John and Stella unload all the luggage. John shot him a glance, which was returned by Declan lifting his small bag and smiling, not moving to help.

Emily was the last to leave the wagon. As she moved to place her foot on the only step, the hem of her dress caught the edge of the seat and she fell—face-first into the thin mud. A loud wailing commenced.

† † †

"What is that awful sound?" said Sdzeè, turning to look out the window and down the street toward the noise. "Sounds like someone is screaming or crying."

Thomas jumped up, caught his left foot in the chair leg, and promptly fell backwards onto the rough lumber floor. Sdzeè grabbed his hand and pulled him up. "Come on. I think the stage is here."

Thomas swung the door of the roadhouse open, stepped out on the landing, and looked down the street. It was them, Stella and John, along with another man, bent over the source of the noise. Suddenly it became clear—it was Emily.

Thomas took off on a run, Sdzeè close behind.

"What happened?" said Thomas.

All eyes turned from Emily. "Thomas!" said Stella. "So glad to see you. Poor Emily fell getting down from the stage, but she won't stand up."

Thomas edged in between John and Stella, and before he could speak, Emily lifted her head, revealing a muddy face streaked with tears, her hair a chocolate brown from the sludge. She started bawling.

"Come on Emily, let's get you up," said Thomas extending his hand. John reached in to help, but before he could lend a hand, a young Indian woman was there, helping Thomas lift Emily from the mud.

Emily made it to her feet, a soaking, disheveled, muddy mess. She continued to cry.

"Are you okay?" said Thomas.

Emily looked at him and then noticed the young woman next to him.

"Who is this?" she asked, the crying abruptly halted and her voice strengthening.

"I am Sdzeè. I am the partner of Thomas."

Thomas winced, knowing that word could be taken in more than one way. Every eye now turned to Thomas, Emily's glare the most piercing.

"Uh...it's a long story," said Thomas.

"Well, I for one want to hear it," said Emily, muddy arms now crossed as she stared at Sdzeè.

"It is not so long. I saved his life. He and I are now partners. He must work for me."

"Of all the gall," said Emily, wiping mud-streaked tears from her face with the back of her hand.

John stepped forward. "Come, lets get you cleaned up and not ruin our reunion. There'll be plenty of time to hear the full story once we make it to the claim."

Emily huffed and turned her back, while John shook both Thomas's and Sdzeè's hand, afterward introducing Declan who stood back, same thin grin on his face. Thomas approached Emily, but the reception remained cold. *What has happened to her?*

"Come here you," said Stella, giving Thomas a big hug. "I've been worried about you."

Sdzeè stepped up and extended her hand, which Stella shook gently. "You are Stella. I have heard many good things of you from Thomas."

"Thank you," said Stella. "Now I should help Emily get cleaned up. Is there a place?"

"The roadhouse has a room you can use. We'll get the wagon loaded," said Thomas.

Stella took hold of Emily's elbow and managed to gently usher her toward the roadhouse.

"Sounds like a lot has been happening in my absence," said John.

"Yes, I'll fill you all in once we get settled. Seems Emily is very mad at me for some reason," said Thomas.

"The trip has been hard on her. She's not much of a frontier girl I'm afraid."

Thomas sighed.

"She'll be okay," said John. "At least I think she will. Let's get our wagon loaded up."

Thomas fetched the wagon from in front of the road-house and pulled up to the livery. He hadn't thought about the fact there would be six passengers and the seat could accommodate three if squeezed together. The rest would have to ride in the back among the bags and trunks. He, John, and Sdzeè loaded the wagon, while Declan, leaning against the wagon, finished his second cigarette.

"John, you drive and have Emily and Stella sit up with you. The rest of us will ride in back," said Thomas.

Declan looked toward Sdzeè. "Is *she* going with us?"

Thomas glared at him, an opinion of his character already forming. He thought about telling him if he didn't like it, he could walk, but thought better of it. "Yes, she is. Any objections?"

Declan didn't say anything, just threw his cigarette into the mud, leaving it smoldering.

"I will be going home once we get to the claim, if it is not too late" said Sdzeè.

Thomas looked at his watch. Already nearly three in the afternoon. *This could be uncomfortable,* he thought as he threw the last bag in the wagon and looked toward the roadhouse.

CHAPTER 10

The trip from town to the claim was uneasy for Thomas. Small talk ensued, with Emily saying little. After many long days on the trail, she was not happy with yet another wagon ride. Thomas wondered what her reaction would be when she saw the small log cabin, the dormitory tent, and most of all, the outhouse. Again he marveled at how different people could be—Stella the strong independent woman running her own business alone, and Sdzeè, a widow living in the wilderness with only a dog team for company. *How different they are from Emily,* he thought.

It was late afternoon when they started up the last hill to the Angel Creek claim. John and Stella were both excited to see what Thomas had done with the place, while Declan seemed uninterested in any of it. Emily remained in a huff, though no longer vocal about it. Now and then she would cast a quick glance back at Sdzeè, sitting next to Thomas on one of the trunks.

John pulled up the reins and stopped the wagon next to the cabin. "Well, this is it—in all its glory," he said.

"Reminds me of my first cabin in Alaska," said Stella. "I must admit though, I've grown accustomed to a frame house," she said, thinking back on her boarding house in Valdez.

Thomas jumped out of the wagon, offered Sdzeè a hand, which she ignored, and began unloading the trunks.

"It's not much, but we'll build a real house this summer," he said.

Everyone was off the wagon except Emily, who stared at Thomas. Finally he looked up and saw her gaze. "Here Emily, let me help you down."

She turned her head away from him, nose a bit in the air, and extended her hand. Thomas helped her down without incident. "Let me show you the cabin."

Thomas opened the door and they entered the dark cabin, their eyes taking a moment to adjust.

Emily took one look at the dirt floor, the crude log bunks, and the rusting, sooty wood stove and said, "Oh, my," followed by a gasp.

"I know it's not what you're used to, but we can make it home," said Thomas.

"We are expected to live here? It's so small—and dirty."

"Like I said, we plan to build a real house. You just have to be patient."

"But there isn't enough room for everyone. And no privacy."

"You and Stella will have the cabin. The rest of us will stay in the dormitory."

"Dormitory?"

"Yes, that large canvas tent with the wood stove. You saw it when we pulled up, didn't you?"

Emily slumped down at the crude table, wiping away the dust. "I guess I did," she said, head in her hands.

"What is wrong? I know it's not much, but we can make the best of it together," said Thomas.

"This is not what I expected. Not at all."

"It's a start. We've got a good chance at—"

Sdzeè burst in the door, bags in hand as she brushed

past Emily and tossed them on the bunk. "Which bunk do you want?"

Emily stared at her, then looked at Thomas. "What do you mean?" she said.

"Which bunk? Upper or lower? I will sleep in a chair."

Emily scowled, her brow wrinkled and lower lip jutting. "What in world are you talking about?"

"You and Stella will each have a bunk," said Thomas.

Emily slowly looked around, the extent of the accommodations finally sinking in. "Oh. There are no real beds."

"Which? I have your bag," said Sdzeè.

Emily didn't look at her, but fixed her stare on Thomas. "Why is she staying with us?"

Thomas looked down, shuffled his feet, and finally looked up. "It's too late for her to make it home before dark. It's not safe, so she will spend the night."

Emily jumped up from the table and stormed toward the door. "Well, I never!"

"Wait," said Thomas, too late as she slammed the door behind her.

† † †

"This is not going to happen," said Emily, arms crossed, staring at her father as he dropped the last bag in the dormitory tent.

"What's not going to happen?"

"We are not having that...that woman living here."

John looked at her, wondering how she could keep her face screwed up in that ugly expression for so long. He smiled. "Who? Stella?"

"You know perfectly well who I mean."

John sat on the edge of one of the cots and looked at her, waiting to see if her demeanor would change. Crossing his legs, he pulled out his pipe and tobacco pouch.

"Aren't you going to say something?" she demanded as she stomped her foot on the wooden floor of the tent platform.

John lit the pipe, took a long draw, and patted the cot next to him. "Sit down, Emily."

"I'll stand," she said, arms still crossed.

"Have it your way." John took another draw on the pipe, then said, "Do you remember—"

Declan entered the tent. "What's going on?" said Declan. "Am I interrupting something?"

"My daughter and I need to have a talk—in private."

"Oh, what about?" said Declan.

John stared at him. "None of your concern. I would appreciate if you would give us some privacy."

Declan ignored him, and looked at Emily, still holding her pose. He smiled and her posture eased, hands dropping to her side. A thin smile formed on her lips.

"Now!" said John.

Declan winked at Emily, turned, and left the tent.

"Why are you mean to him?" said Emily.

John ignored the question. "Do you remember when you were having trouble in school years ago?"

Emily shook her head. "Yes, but what does that have to do with anything?"

"You were butting heads with the teacher, doing things your own way because you thought you knew better."

"I remember. So?"

"Back then I gave you some advice that would serve

you well now."

"I don't remember."

John sighed. "I told you to stop swimming upstream and go with the flow—to stop being so stubborn."

She crossed her arms again. "I'm sorry I'm such a disappointment to you."

So am I, thought John, but didn't utter it. "That's not it. You need to relax and go with the flow here. We're all just trying to adjust and you being in a snit all the time makes it hard on everyone, not just you."

Emily stared at the floor.

"I know it's been hard on you with all that has happened in the last year, but you have to realize we're all going through a lot of changes. We need to help each other and be as positive as we can," said John.

"I don't like her," said Emily.

"Why?"

"She has designs on Thomas. I can tell."

"I haven't seen any sign of that—just a person willing to help."

"You aren't looking very hard," said Emily.

"You should thank her."

Emily huffed. "Thank her? Are you serious?"

"Ask Thomas. You don't know all that has gone on here in the last few weeks."

"I'm sure I don't," said Emily, crossing her arms once again.

John stood. "We need to get settled before nightfall. I suggest you go to the cabin and organize your things."

Without a word, Emily whirled and ducked out of the tent. John sat back down, took off his hat, and took a long draw on his pipe.

† † †

Stella and Sdzeè were sitting at the table when Emily finally returned to the cabin. The wood stove was cranking out heat, making it nearly too warm. There was a pot of something bubbling on the stove. Thomas was gone. She looked around, then moved past the table to the bunks. Her bags were sitting on the top bunk. She turned and looked back at the table. Sdzeè smiled, but said nothing. Emily opened a bag and began rustling through it without much purpose. *Where's Thomas?*

"Are you hungry?" said Stella. "I've got a stew started."

Emily turned and stared at her. "I see you wasted no time getting domestic."

Stella raised her eyebrows. "It's what I do," she said flatly.

"I'm not hungry." She looked squarely at Sdzeè. "Where's Thomas?"

"He went to get wood for the night," said Sdzeè. "It will be cold tonight."

Stella got up to tend to the stew. Emily continued to fuss with her bunk and bags, occasionally glancing at Sdzeè who remained seated and unfazed.

"Emily, will you go and tell the others the stew is ready?"

"I said I'm not hungry."

Stella stopped stirring. "I know you're not. But everyone else is. Now please—"

Sdzeè popped up from the table and headed to the door. "I will go," she said as she left the cabin.

Stella just stood there, wooden spoon at her side, looking at Emily.

"I'm glad she went. Why is she here? I don't like her," said Emily in rapid fashion.

"You have no reason to dislike her."

"I don't understand why I'm the only one that sees it."

"Sees what?"

"That she is after Thomas."

Stella returned to stirring. "Ah, I see. You're jealous."

"I have a right to be. Who knows what has been going on here."

"Have you asked Thomas?"

Emily crossed her arms. "No, I—"

The door opened and Sdzeè entered, followed by Thomas carrying a huge load of firewood in his arms. Sdzeè shut the door and helped Thomas stack the wood by the stove, then sat down at the table.

"Where's the rest of them?" said Stella.

"They are coming quickly," said Sdzeè.

"It's going to be a bit crowded in here," said Thomas.

"Yes, I agree," said Emily, turning to look directly at one seated at the table.

"We'll get by," said Stella. "Thomas, do you have plates handy?"

"I'll get them."

Declan entered the cabin, followed by John. With six people in the one room cabin, things were cozy. The table had room for four, as long as everyone could put up with some knee-bumping. That meant the others had to sit on the lower bunk to eat. Emily avoided the table and sat on the bunk, waiting. Thomas looked around, then took a seat at the table. Emily frowned, though no one paid attention.

Stella scooped stew onto the tin plates and passed them around. John handed one to Emily, then sat next to her. Declan was already eating, not waiting for anyone.

"Wait," said Stella.

Declan looked up, mouth full. "Huh?" he mumbled.

"I think we should say a prayer for this meal and for the providence provided on our trip."

No one said anything. Declan stared at his plate, slowly chewing a mouthful. Stella waited. She looked at Thomas. She turned to John—waiting.

"Why don't you do it, dear?" said John.

"Bow your heads," said Stella. "And put down that spoon, Declan."

"Yes, ma'am."

Stella prayed, thanking God for protection and, despite the mishaps along the way, a safe journey. Lastly, she blessed the food.

"Amen. Now eat," she said.

Emily picked at her food, occasionally glancing toward the table, but mostly staring at her plate. For the longest time, the only sound was the crackling of the fire in the wood stove.

Declan broke the silence. "So, what's the plan?"

"Well, we've got a lot to do, both at the mine and around the camp," said Thomas. He went on to describe the daily mine chore of building a fire, thawing gravel, then hoisting it to the surface the next day. Though the snow was rapidly melting with a few patches remaining, the creek was just starting to thaw. This meant there wasn't enough water to begin sluicing—besides that, the pile of gravel Thomas hoisted over the winter was still largely frozen.

"We also want to upgrade the living quarters," said John. "Have any carpenter experience, Declan?"

"I'm afraid not."

"What experience do you have?" asked Thomas.

Declan smiled. "Well, I know how to cheat at poker."

Thomas wondered about him. *Was he serious?*

"Well, I hope you're a quick learner," said John. "Because we don't have time to get you up to speed."

Declan leaned back in the chair and began rolling a cigarette.

"Do not forget your other job, Thomas," said Sdzeè.

Emily dropped the spoon on her plate. "What job?"

Sdzeè smiled at her. "Thomas must mine for me."

Emily huffed. "What?" she said, her voice shrill.

Sdzeè's smile didn't fade. "I think it is time you told a story, Thomas."

Thomas nodded. Perhaps an explanation would calm Emily's demeanor, especially when she heard that without Sdzeè, he wouldn't be here.

Thomas began. "Well, I was out trapping along the Mosquito Fork..."

He went on to relate the whole story—how he fell through the ice and Sdzeè saved him from freezing to death. Sdzeè chimed in and told of her husband's death and the plan to reopen her mine.

"I see," said Emily. "And what's in it for him?"

"Emily," her father said sternly.

Sdzeè smiled. "Thomas is my partner."

"Partner?" said Declan.

"I have given him half interest in my mine," said Sdzeè.

Emily looked hard at Sdzeè. This wasn't a business deal—she was convinced this was just a ploy to spirit Thomas away—to keep him away from her. "How is he supposed to work for you and work here?" she said, turning to Thomas.

"I guess I'll be pretty busy."

Emily looked at John. "Father?"

"We'll figure it out. After all, we have one extra hand and it is another opportunity. We'll make it work somehow."

Thomas went on to describe the plan for Sdzeè's mine, as well as the plans to build a frame house as soon as possible. Everyone agreed it was a lot of work. Stella and John were optimistic—Declan and Emily not so much.

Thomas and John laid out the plan for the next few days. Since sluicing wasn't an option, they would focus on the thawing/hoisting operation, while beginning work on Sdzeè's new mine entrance. Once breakup was complete, they would shift to laying out the site for the new house and beginning construction. For now, they would focus on the mine operations.

"And what am I to do all day?" said Emily.

"Help Stella wherever you can. It will be up to you two to keep us fed," said John.

Declan took a long, last drag on his cigarette, then threw it smoldering on the dirt floor. "And me?"

John looked at the smoldering butt, then at Declan. "You're in for the time of your life, son. We're going to turn you into a miner."

† † †

CHAPTER 11

Sdzeè left just before first light to return to her cabin. Emily was still in bed when she departed, but rose enough to watch her quietly gather her things and tiptoe out the door, whispering a goodbye to Stella who was already busy preparing coffee. Emily closed her eyes, glad to see her go.

The men filtered in one by one, forcing Emily to hide under the covers. Stella had already taken inventory of the supplies and made a note as to what they would need before long. Thomas hadn't stocked up to support four additional mouths to feed. Someone would have to make a supply run to town soon.

Declan was the last to enter the cabin. Thomas and John were already on their second cup of coffee when he came in, cigarette hanging from his mouth. He plopped down at the table and Stella set a steaming cup of black coffee in front of him.

"What? No cream?" he said.

Thomas laughed. "Not here. I haven't seen a cow all winter."

Declan snorted and took a sip. Stella freshened up the cups all around, then returned to the rough wood counter next to the stove. She turned back with her list of supplies and handed it to John.

"We're going to need these things soon," she said.

John looked at the list, which included staples like flour, salt pork, beans, and most of all coffee. "We can probably get most of this at the store, but supplies might be running thin there after the long winter."

"We'll make do with what you can get," said Stella.

Emily, now propped up on one elbow and looking down on the scene, let out a big yawn.

"Why are you still in bed?" said John. "From now on, you'll get up when Stella does."

Emily started to protest but stopped, groaned once, and pulled the covers over her head.

The crackling smell of fried potatoes filled the cabin as Stella worked to prepare breakfast. Thomas turned to Declan, "After we eat, get your warm coat on. We'll be going down to the mine to haul out some gravel."

Declan grunted and took a gulp of coffee.

"Thomas, how are we fixed for funds?" said John.

"Pretty sure we have enough gold to keep us in beans and maybe get started on the frame house, but not enough to do everything I want," said Thomas.

"What else?" said John.

"If we're ever going to make a real go of this, we need a steam boiler, a hoist, and some steam points."

"Steam points?" said Declan.

"Yes, with them we can thaw the gravel much faster than building a wood fire and letting it sit overnight. That will increase our productivity immensely."

"Not to mention help in sinking the shaft on Sdzeè's claim," said John.

Emily huffed at the sound of her name, causing all but Declan to look up at her, still under the covers.

"Maybe once we sluice the gravel from the winter we'll be able to purchase some used equipment. Surely there must be some laying around on a claim somewhere in the district," said Thomas.

"Let's keep an eye out—maybe we can work a deal to borrow or make payments," said John.

Stella set plates on the table, steaming with fried salt pork and potatoes. "Eat up boys, it's a long time till dinner," she said, smiling as she returned to tending the stove.

† † †

Declan stood, leaning on the shovel as he watched Thomas swing away with the pick. The ground was partially frozen—with all that was going on, Thomas had waited too long to tend to it. With each swing of the pick, melon-sized chunks of half-frozen gravel flew from the face of the drift.

Though it was near thirty degrees in the mine, Thomas quickly worked up a sweat. He paused, removed his coat, and laid it aside, then looked at Declan, resting comfortably on the end of the shovel. *Let's see if this boy can work.*

"Load up those buckets while I take a breather," said Thomas.

Declan looked at the clods of half-frozen gravel. "Is there really gold in this stuff?"

"Yes, there's gold. You'll see that when we start sluicing."

Declan picked up a clod and turned it over in his hands, peering closely. "I don't see any," he said as he crumbled it, pieces falling to the floor of the drift.

"It's in there—trust me. But it doesn't do any good down here. We need to get it to the surface if we're going to get any gold."

Declan grunted and halfheartedly began to fill the buckets. Thomas watched, noting he would have filled them and had them halfway up the shaft in the time it took Declan to get half a bucket full. *Too bad he didn't come with references.*

Thomas went back to swinging the pick and before long the loud clang of frozen solid gravel filled the drift. "Guess that's all we'll get today. Let's get what we have up to the surface, then we'll build a fire."

Declan picked up the half-filled buckets and started toward the shaft.

"Wait!" said Thomas. "Let's fill those full, otherwise we're going to be here half the day."

Declan turned slowly, his face wrinkled, then returned to the gravel pile, dropping the buckets. Thomas shook his head.

"I'll fill them, you shuttle them to the shaft, then we'll hoist them all at once."

Declan nodded and gave Thomas a glimmer of hope that gravel would make it to the surface before dinner. If only they had real equipment—side-dump rail cars, a steam-powered hoist, steam points—then they could really do something. Thomas envisioned it all as he shoveled, filling the buckets while Declan waited.

Most of the winter Thomas had done everything by himself. To get the gravel to the surface he had to manually hoist the buckets, two at a time, then tie off the rope while he climbed to the surface. Then the buckets were unhooked, carried to the pile, and dumped. It was time-consuming, but now with two working, it should go faster—at least Thomas hoped it would.

Thomas instructed Declan on the process. "You go to the top, and I'll hoist the buckets up. Unhook and dump them on the pile while I hoist the next load."

Declan put one hand on the ladder, then just looked at him with a frown. Thomas wasn't sure what he was thinking, but having worked with him for just a short time, he got the distinct impression that Declan didn't like being told what to do.

"Okay," said Declan as he climbed the ladder.

The process went fairly quickly, giving Thomas hope that their new hand might actually work out. "That's it," said Thomas after the last buckets were hoisted. "I'm coming up."

Thomas waited until Declan removed the buckets before he started the climb up the ladder. He heard the story of more than one drift miner sent to the great beyond by a falling bucket. Reaching the top, he saw Declan dumping the last bucket in a new pile that was far too close to the shaft. He cursed under his breath.

"Done," said Declan, unceremoniously dropping the bucket with a clang.

Thomas crossed his arms. "Do you see that big pile of gravel over there?"

Declan looked, then nodded.

"That's where we dump the gravel, not next to the shaft."

"Should've been more specific," said Declan as he took a pouch from his vest pocket and began rolling a cigarette.

The veins in Thomas's forehead bulged, the urge to slap the pouch from Declan's hands nearly uncontrollable. That, of course, would lead to more slapping, perhaps punching, and maybe even a real knock-down, drag-out fight. He resisted.

"I was specific, but perhaps you misunderstood me," said Thomas, knowing that wasn't the real issue. "Get a

wheelbarrow and a shovel and move it where it belongs,"
said Thomas calmly.

Declan looked at him and smiled, then lit his cigarette.
"I'll do it later," he said as he walked off, headed toward
the cabin.

Good thing I don't have the carbine with me, thought
Thomas in jest as he watched him go. *I have to talk to
John.*

† † †

John and Stella returned from the supply run to town
about the time Thomas finished up at the mine. He heard
the wagon coming as he climbed out of the shaft and
worked to replace the cover. Even though it was still cold
at night, he didn't want to risk any thawing, especially at
the top of the shaft. Finished, he trudged up to the cabin,
all the while wondering what happened to his wayward
helper.

"Get everything?" said Thomas as he reached the wagon.

"Most of it," said Stella. "It's not quite the same as
old Noel's store in Valdez."

"That's for sure," said John.

Thomas grabbed one box from the wagon, John taking the other. In the cabin they found Declan and Emily
sitting at the table, chatting. They stopped when the
group entered.

Thomas sat the box on the counter next to the stove.
"What are you talking about?"

Declan looked at Emily and smiled, then put out his
cigarette. "Nothing."

"Must be a pretty boring conversation, talking about
nothing," said John as he helped unload the boxes.

"I can take care of this," said Stella. "I'm sure you have better things to do."

Thomas moved toward the door. "John, I need to talk to you and Declan. In the tent."

"Now?" said Declan.

"Yes, now," said Thomas as he opened the door.

† † †

Thomas looked at Declan, sitting on one of the cots, yet another cigarette hanging from his mouth.

"Why are you here?" said Thomas.

Declan glanced at John. "Ask him. He knows."

John crossed his arms and waited. Thomas stared. Declan's knee began to bounce up and down ever so slightly. He took a drag on his cigarette and blew the smoke out slowly.

"Here to work," he said finally.

"Well, why don't you explain today for me."

"What do you mean?"

"You walked off after I told you to move the gravel to the dump."

"I said I'd do it later."

"I don't know who you've worked for in the past, but when I tell you to do something, you do it. This isn't a partnership—you're a hired hand."

"Working for nothing," said Declan.

"That's not true—you're getting room and board and as far as I know, John agreed to pay you a wage."

John nodded. "Stella said you'd work for free but we agreed to pay you something, depending on how the season went."

"I see," said Declan.

"It's beside the point," said Thomas. "You wanted to come and said you'd work. If that's true, I'm willing to give you a shot. If not, pack up now and be on your way."

Declan looked to John, hoping for an ally, but found nothing on his face to indicate it. He stood up and crushed out his cigarette. "Okay, we'll do it your way," he said as he walked out of the tent.

Thomas shook his head and looked at John. "How did we end up with this guy?"

"Stella had pity on him," said John. "If it were up to me, he wouldn't be here. I haven't cared for him from the start."

"How long do we carry him?"

John rubbed his chin. "Until he works out or I get the courage to tell Stella he has to go."

CHAPTER 12

It was in the mid 30's when Thomas rolled off his cot. The wood stove in the dorm tent had nearly gone cold, only a few embers living. He buttoned up his shirt, pulled on his pants, then sat on the edge of his cot. He could hear the muffled breathing of John and Declan, both still sleeping. He pulled out his pocket watch. *Six o'clock.*

Thomas laced up his boots quietly, thought about stoking the stove, but decided against it. His guess was that Stella was already up. He thought he could smell coffee wafting on the air, but knew it was his imagination. *Couldn't smell it from here.*

He slipped quietly out of the tent and made his way through the darkness to the cabin. With Emily and Stella bunking in the cabin, he was wary of just walking in. Pausing outside the door, he listened, hoping to hear the sound of coffee being brewed. Thomas stuck his hands in the pocket of his pants and shivered, having left his coat in the tent. He was about to turn and head back to the tent when he heard a noise from inside the cabin. He knocked ever so gently and waited.

The door creaked open and Stella peered out. "Oh, Thomas, come in. Coffee's ready and we're up."

Thomas was surprised to hear Emily was already up, but there she was, seated at the table with a cup of coffee in front of her. She didn't look up when he entered, but rather continued to stare blankly at the cup. Her hair was a tangled mess, her clothes wrinkled and smudged. She looked nothing like the young girl Thomas met on the docks of Seattle years ago. *She has changed, in more ways than one,* thought Thomas.

"Good Morning, Emily."

She looked up. "Is it?"

"Another beautiful day in paradise," said Thomas cheerfully.

Emily just sighed, put her hands around the coffee cup, looked down.

"What's wrong?" said Thomas, immediately realizing he may have opened the proverbial can of worms.

Emily looked up, her brow knitted. "What do you think, Thomas?"

"Look, I know things are different than Valdez, but we're going to—"

"This place is awful!" she said, raising her voice. "I had no idea we were coming to the end of the earth to live in a cave of a cabin, with dirt floors and log furniture. Plus I have to be around your new friend that obviously is in love with you."

Thomas's mouth dropped for an instant. "I have no idea what you're talking about."

"Sdzeè—she's in love with you pure and simple," said Emily.

"That's ridiculous. She saved my life and has been a great help getting things ready for you to arrive. A friend—nothing more."

"I don't believe you. Declan has paid more attention to me since we got here than you have."

"Yes, I've noticed," said Thomas dryly.

"I don't want to see that woman around here again. I

won't have it."

Thomas stared at her, the words not coming—at least none he dare say.

"Emily, I think you're making too much of this," said Stella. "Sdzeè is just being a good neighbor, plus she's been good enough to give Thomas a fifty-percent stake in her mine."

"I don't care. She's a tramp."

"Don't you dare call her that," said Thomas. "You better shape up and get used to things around here. Sdzeè is a part of things now and you'll just have to learn to live with it."

Emily glared, picked up the cup of coffee, and threw it at Thomas. He dodged, and it bounced off the cabin door, the contents soaking into the dirt floor.

"I'm done with you," said Thomas as he swung the door open and left the cabin.

Emily stared at the door, then broke down, sobbing incessantly, her head in her hands, elbows on the table.

"You handled that poorly," said Stella as she picked up the cup.

"I don't need your opinion," she said, straightening up.

"What has gotten into you? You're like a different person since we left Valdez."

"I don't want to be here. Thomas has betrayed me. Betrayed our engagement."

"That's all in your head—I've seen no evidence."

"Why am I the only one that sees it?" said Emily, her voice breaking.

"Because you are jealous and overreacting," said Stella.

"I thought you were on my side."

Stella didn't answer—arguing with her was pointless

when she was in a mood.

"Well?" said Emily.

Stella pulled the cast iron skillet from the shelf and placed it on the stove. "I have to get breakfast going," she said. "Just give things a chance, Emily."

† † †

Breakfast was a muted affair with little conversation. Stella let John know about the early morning conflict, hoping he had a solution, but things remained up in the air.

Stella cleared the last of the plates and finally broke the silence. "What's the plan for today?"

Thomas looked at Emily, then to John as if to encourage him to speak up.

"Well," said John, "Since there's still ice along the creek it's too early to set up the sluice boxes here, so we're going over to Sdzeè's claim and see about starting on the new shaft."

Emily rolled her eyes and shook her head. "Who's we?"

"Us men, but you can go with us if you like," said John.

"No thanks. I don't want to get anywhere near that woman."

Thomas stood from the table and opened the door. "I'm going to get the tools together," he said as he left.

"See," said Emily. "He doesn't want to admit that—"

"Emily, let's not go there now," said Stella.

She stopped and looked at Declan who was sitting across from her, a thin grin on his face. He winked. She looked away, then looked back.

"Come on Declan, let's get going," said John.

"When will you be back?" said Stella.

"Not sure," said John. "Depends on how things go, but we'll definitely be home for supper. Don't want to miss out on your good cooking."

Stella smiled and kissed him on the forehead. Then returned to the breakfast dishes.

"Sure you don't want to come along?" said Declan. "Might be fun."

Emily huffed. "I'll stay here in this miserable place."

It was about six miles from the claim to Sdzeè's place. The route took them down Chicken Creek to town, then west along the Valdez-Eagle trail to the Mosquito Fork. From there, a narrow trail skirted the river westward to her claim that sat on a small tributary. Thomas drove the wagon with John next to him and Declan lounging in the back, smoking an endless stream of cigarettes.

"I don't think we'll get much done today," said Thomas. "Maybe get the site laid out and start a thaw fire once we dig down to frozen ground."

"How much digging is that?" said Declan.

"Around here the permafrost is not too far below the surface. This time of year I doubt the ground has thawed much at all. Biggest chore will be hauling wood and getting a good fire going."

"Sounds fun," said Declan, flicking his smoldering cigarette into the brush along the trail.

There was little traffic on the trail and the condition was improved from just a few days ago, allowing them to make good time. Thomas expected Declan to be full of questions, but he was content to recline in the back of the wagon, often not even looking.

"How much further?" said John.

"Oh, I forgot you haven't been here—we're almost there," said Thomas. "So much has been going on I'm a bit rummy sometimes."

John laughed. "I'm with you there. I think it's going to be a while before things settle down, if you know what I mean."

"I know what he means," chimed Declan, which caused Thomas to shoot him a quick glance.

They rounded a bend on the narrow trail and a cabin came into view. It was a bit larger than theirs, but of similar construction. Smoke whispered from the chimney. A dog sled was parked neatly beside the cabin and as they approached, the sound of barking dogs met their ears.

"What in the world is that?" said Declan.

"That's Sdzeè's dog team welcoming us. No sneaking up on her," said Thomas.

"How many does she have?"

"Not sure," said Thomas. "Eight or ten I think."

"Must be a chore to take care of them," said Declan.

"Yes, but it's worth it to have them in the winter."

The cabin door opened and Sdzeè stepped out, followed by an enormous dog. She waved and motioned for them to pull up next to the cabin.

"Hello, Sdzeè," said Thomas.

"Hello, Thomas Thornton." She put her hands on her hips and looked squarely at them. "Are you ready to work?" She stared for a moment, expression firm, then broke into a laugh.

"That's why we're here," said John.

Thomas patted the horse, then tied it off to a nearby tree. "Get the tools Declan, it's a bit of walk to the mine site."

The trail from the cabin to the mine was deeply rutted. Thomas wondered if the wagon could even make it without bottoming out. Eventually they would need to get the wagon up there to bring in needed timber and supplies. The trail would probably need some work. *Maybe a good job for Declan.*

They slogged along the trail through the mud, tools in hand, passing a small shed just before they reached the caved shaft. The snow had greatly retreated since Thomas's initial visit, and though the trail was clear, some large patches of snow remained.

"We'll start here," said Thomas, moving through the ankle-deep snow to the spot he and Sdzeè located previously.

"Here?" said Declan, looking at the snow-covered ground.

"Start digging," said Thomas as he used his shovel to outline a square area in the snow.

Declan began moving the snow, exposing the frozen tundra underneath. He worked slowly—so much so that John pitched in to help. With the snow out of the way, Thomas took a pick and swung hard at the ground. It penetrated the frozen vegetation, then stopped with a dull thud. He flipped the pick over and swung again, tearing up a small patch of tundra when he pried the handle back.

"No reason to expect that we'd find thawed ground," said Thomas. "We should have brought more than one pick to hack this tundra away."

"There are tools in the shed," said Sdzeè. "Come."

Thomas handed his pick to Declan and followed Sdzeè to the shed, a short distance away. The shed wasn't locked but had a hasp on the double doors. A short piece of caribou antler served as a pin to keep the hasp secure. Sdzeè removed the antler and swung the doors open. Thomas took a step back, mouth agape. There in the shed sat a small steam boiler still bolted to 4x6 wooden skids and surrounded by piping and what Thomas could only assume were steam points. He let out a whoop.

"I didn't know you had this!" said Thomas.

Sdzeè looked surprised. "It has never been used. My husband bought it from a miner leaving the country and planned to put it to use, but it was not to be."

"Do you know how much easier this will make our job? Instead of taking overnight to thaw a foot of gravel with a wood fire, we can thaw that much in an hour or less."

"Do you know how to put it together?"

"It's simple I think. Looks like everything we need is here, except for wood and water to feed the boiler."

The others heard the commotion and now stood behind Thomas, looking at the new-found equipment. John recognized the value of the find—Declan had no idea what the excitement was about.

Thomas was talking excitedly about how the boiler was going to speed things up dramatically, the need for water, and of course the need for lots of wood to keep it running. To Declan, it just sounded like more work.

John looked around, wondering where they would find the wood. Water was no problem—the creek wasn't too far away. The valley, however, was sparsely timbered, rather than a dense forest. Seasoned wood was the best burning, but there didn't seem to be a supply of that nearby, apart from what Sdzeè had stockpiled for heating her cabin. A mixture of black spruce and poplar could be found in more abundance lower in the valley.

"Going to be a chore keeping that thing fed with wood," said John.

"Well, we would have needed wood for thaw fires anyway, so it's not that much different," said Thomas. "The biggest issue is getting a wagon load of logs up here."

Sdzeè smiled at their words. "I have a suggestion."

John and Thomas looked at her, waiting.

"We do not need to get the wagon up here, just use your horse to skid the logs, then we can buck them up here for the boiler."

Declan laughed out loud. "She's got you there."

Thomas nudged the horse one more time, finally skidding the boiler to the spot they had cleared for it. It was close to the site of the new shaft—but not too close. Now that it was in place, he stood looking at it, rubbing his chin.

"What is the matter?" said Sdzeè.

"Well, I'm wondering what happens when the boiler heats up the ground underneath it and it starts thawing."

"It will sink," she said matter-of-factly. "The ground is frozen silt. When it thaws it turns into muck. You can hardly pull your boot from it."

"Exactly," said Thomas.

"So what do we do?" she said.

"Maybe we should move it down along the creek where there is gravel instead of muck. It would make it easier to keep it stocked with water, the only question is whether we have enough hose to reach the site."

Sdzeè started off on a trot to the shed where the steam points were. "Let us find out."

Thomas finally caught up to her and took inventory of the equipment. There were two coils of hose for running from the boiler to the steam points. Under them lay two brand new steam points. Thomas pulled one out and looked at it. The steam point was about five feet long with a chisel point at the bottom and a driving plate on the top. A hose attachment was located near the top.

"This seems simple enough," he said.

Sdzeè gave him a look. "You are supposed to be checking the hose to see if it will work."

"Oh, sorry," he said as he slung a coil of hose over his shoulder, straining under the weight. "Let's take it to the site and unroll it toward the creek to see how far we get."

He trudged to the site, then dropped the hose. "Help me unroll it," he said. "Should've had the others here to help with setting all this up I guess."

"Yes, but they are cutting wood which we need."

"True," said Thomas.

Declan and John had gone down the valley to collect wood. Thomas told them to look for standing dead trees that would burn well.

After unrolling the hose and reaching the creek, Thomas estimated they still had twenty or thirty feet remaining. *That's good news*, thought Thomas. There was plenty of hose length to sink the shaft and began drifting to intersect the old workings.

"Let's get the boiler in place so we can take the horse down to fetch the wood," said Thomas.

Sdzeè nodded and helped Thomas rig the ropes needed to move the boiler.

The horse didn't seem particularly happy about skidding the boiler down the slope to the creek, but Thomas gently persuaded her along the way. He found a level spot about ten feet from the active channel and unhooked the horse. The boiler was nearly level and with a bit of shovel work, he and Sdzeè were able to trim it up. Now all that remained was charging it with water and getting a fire going—that and figuring out how to properly regulate the pressure without blowing something up.

"Let's take the horse down and see how John's getting along," said Thomas. "We're going to need some wood—water's no problem now."

Sdzeè took the lead and headed for the trail down the valley.

"Wait for me," said Thomas.

Sdzeè stopped and looked at him, saying nothing.

"What?"

"You stay here and get everything ready for the boiler. I want to see it work today," said Sdzeè.

"But I—"

"No. Today I am boss. We can handle bringing the wood up. Today you are chief mining engineer," she said, her face rigid, eyes narrowed.

"I'm no mining engineer, but—"

Sdzeè roared with laughter. "You take everything too seriously. I will be back soon." She turned and continued on. "Please get the boiler ready."

"Alright," he shouted. "I'll do as ordered."

† † †

It took Thomas about an hour to run the hose line from the boiler to the site and hook everything up. Though there were two steam points, there wasn't a means to attach both of them at once. They were missing a needed T-connection. He filled the boiler with water and looked around for something to get a fire started, hoping to get a jump on things. For a moment he thought about "borrow-ing" some of Sdzeè's firewood at the cabin but decided against it. He returned to the shaft site and jabbed the cold steam point into the ground. The chisel point pene-trated an inch or so. *Nothing left to do but wait for wood.*

Thomas finished his cigarette and crushed it out with his foot. He decided to go find the others and see if he could help. He got about ten feet from the boiler when he heard Sdzeè's voice, urging the horse on. They came into view, Sdzeè leading the log-skidding horse. John and Declan followed behind the bundle of small diame-ter black spruce, each no more than five inches in diam-eter. John had the whipsaw slung over one shoulder and it flexed up and down as he walked.

"That'll get us started," said Thomas. "We're going to have to cut it to length though—too long to get in the firebox."

Declan groaned. "More sawing?"

Sdzeè ignored him. "There is a sawbuck at the cabin. If someone gets it we can whipsaw up a bunch of wood quickly."

Thomas looked at Declan. "You know what a saw-buck is?"

"Not really."

"It's got boards sticking up at each end that form an 'X'. You lay the log across to hold it while we cut," said Thomas.

"Except mine is made from spruce poles, not lum-ber," said Sdzeè.

"Think you can find it now?"

"Probably," said Declan.

"Well hustle, and bring back some dry kindling to get the fire going."

Declan looked puzzled. "You want me to go cut more wood?"

Sdzeè laughed at him. "No, there is some small split wood in the box next to the firewood pile. Bring some of it."

Declan's eyes narrowed, and the vein on his forehead pulsated. He opened his mouth to speak, then turned and started toward the cabin.

When he was out of earshot, John said, "I haven't figured that guy out yet."

"Me neither," said Thomas.

Sdzeè said nothing, but from the look on her face, Thomas knew she had an opinion. He didn't ask her.

Declan returned a few minutes later, dragging the sawbuck behind him, a bundle of kindling cradled in his left arm. He stopped next to the pile of wood and tossed the kindling on the damp ground.

Thomas frowned, shook his head, and picked up the kindling. John already had a log unbundled and cradled in the sawbuck. He picked up the whipsaw and pointed to Declan. "Get on the other end of the saw, boy. Let's make some logs."

Declan shuffled to the sawbuck and halfheartedly took hold of the opposite end of the eight-foot long saw. John pulled it back to get the cut started, then pushed toward Declan. Declan pushed too, stopping all progress.

John huffed, let go of the saw, and stared at him. "I thought we went over this several times already down in the valley. I push, you pull. You push, I pull. That's how the saw works."

Declan let go, pulled out his tobacco pouch, and started rolling a cigarette. "I'm kind of tired," he said.

Sdzeè jumped in, grabbed the saw, and began making quick work of the cut. John grabbed his end on the backstroke and helped.

"I do this by myself all summer to get my winter wood ready. It is really quite simple," she said.

"Hmph," said Declan as he continued to watch. "I might get it after a few more lessons."

Thomas balled up his fist, but no one noticed. He relaxed, then picked up two of the logs already cut. "I'm going to get the fire started."

He placed the kindling in the firebox, neatly making a teepee of the sticks, realizing the odds of getting the fire going weren't good. He took one of the sticks, pulled out his pocket knife, and begin whittling off shavings. They curled as he sliced each one. It took a while, but before long he had a nice pile of curly fire starter. He was about to light it when Sdzeè stopped him.

"Don't you think we should split some of the logs first?" she said.

"Right," said Thomas. "I'll get an axe."

"There is one in the tool shed," said Sdzeè.

Thomas fetched the axe and split the logs in short order, placing each on the wooden skid of the boiler as he worked.

"Gonna mess that up," said Declan, pointing at the skid.

"Better that than splitting on the ground and dulling the axe each time," said Thomas.

Declan shrugged his shoulders. "Hmph."

Thomas ignored him and placed the split wood in the firebox, careful not to disturb the teepee of kindling and shavings. He pulled a match from the box in his vest pocket and lit the shavings. They glowed but produced no flame. He gently blew on them and a small lick of fire jumped from the cuttings. He continued to nurse the fledgling inferno until the kindling began to crackle. Once he was satisfied it was going to take off, he shut the firebox door and adjusted the damper on the flue. Through the thick sheet of mica that served as a window into the firebox, Thomas could see the flames slowly growing. "I think we have a fire."

The sound of the whipsaw ceased. Sdzeè and John had cut several of the poles up in short order and there was enough wood to keep the boiler going for a while. John motioned for Declan to take up the other end of the saw, then proceeded with another training attempt. Sdzeè inspected the fire.

"I wonder how long it will take to make steam?" she said.

"Probably going to be a while, said Thomas. That water is barely above freezing and it's not that warm out yet. We'll watch the pressure gauge and that should tell us."

"What are we going to do when it gets up to pressure?" said Declan over the noise of the saw.

"Thaw gravel, what else?" said Thomas.

† † †

It took longer than expected for the boiler to begin to make steam. Thomas opened and closed the pressure relief valve several times hoping to see some steam. Eventually, a wisp appeared and the pressure gauge started to climb. Thomas clambered up the slope to the steam point and slowly opened the valve. Steam came shooting out with more pressure than he expected. He pushed the point into the frozen muck, making a little headway. He hollered at John to fetch a sledgehammer.

The hissing of the steam point was loud, making it somewhat hard to hear. Thomas motioned for John to start driving the point with the hammer while he held the point vertical. With each swing of the hammer, the point sank further into the ground. John was able to drive it about a foot before encountering too much resistance.

"Let's leave it there for a bit and see if it thaws around it," said Thomas.

He looked back at the boiler and Sdzeè was waving both arms over her head. Thomas ran down the hill as quickly as he could.

"What's wrong?"

"Is the pressure too high?" she said, pointing at the gauge.

Thomas looked. "No, it's fine. See the red line here?" he said, pointing at the gauge.

Sdzeè nodded.

"If it gets that high we need to worry, although the relief valve will let go before it explodes."

Sdzeè laughed. "That is good news."

Thomas opened the firebox and threw a couple more logs in, this time without splitting them, then returned to the thawing operation. Scratching around with a shovel he found that the ground was thawing slowly, but the area affected was pretty small. It was faster than building a fire on the ground and waiting hours and hours, but still slower than Thomas hoped.

Thomas yelled at John. "We need to get that other point going."

"That's going to require a trip to town or begging off of another mine."

"Frank has a big thaw operation over at his mine. I think I'll ride over there when I get a chance and see if he has anything to spare," said Thomas.

"Good idea," said John. "Let's see how far we can get today."

Thomas shook his head in agreement, then motioned for Sdzeè to come up and have a look. Though they had only scratched the surface, she was pleased with the start.

"There's one thing we need to do, and that's cover the area when we're done for the day," said Thomas. "Even though it's not that warm yet, it will be and we risk thawing and sloughing the sides of the shaft."

Sdzeè nodded. "We will need supplies to build a cover."

"Straw would be best to insulate it with, but I doubt we'll find any in town."

"Moss will work," said Sdzeè. "Or sawdust from the mill."

Thomas agreed. "We're going to need a lot more timber as well—to support the shaft as we go down."

Sdzeè looked down the hill at Declan, leaning up against the sawbuck and smoking another cigarette. "Maybe we can get Declan to cut wood for us," she said—then laughed out loud.

CHAPTER 13

John climbed up the ladder from the fledgling shaft, a bucket of thawed muck in hand. The operation was only three days old and already the shaft was deep enough to require a ladder to access. They were down nearly six feet, but the shaft was narrower than needed. Since it was still fairly cold, the shaft walls were standing well and no cribbing was needed. Still, progress was slow with only one steam point. John handed the bucket to Declan who carried it to the dump and emptied it.

"I hope Thomas has some luck finding the fittings we need to get the other steam point rigged," said John.

Sdzeè nodded. "It would be of help."

"We really need a way to hoist the thawed material up," said John. "This hauling it up a ladder in a bucket is already getting old."

"We need a windlass," said Sdzeè. "I have seen them at other mines—or better, a hoist."

"Hoist?" said Declan as he returned with the empty bucket.

"Yes," said Sdzeè. "Steam-powered with cables to bring up the gravel."

John rubbed his chin and looked down the hole. "Should've mentioned that to Thomas before he went on the hunt."

† † †

Thomas left the mine on Meyers Fork empty-handed. So far he had visited three drift mines, none of which had any spare parts for steam points. Frank's mine was last on his list, only because it was the farthest away and he originally hoped to find what he needed closer.

Frank waved at him as he rode up.

"How are things going for you, Thomas? I heard you have a lot of new faces in camp."

"Yes, it's been pretty busy. There's five of us now at the mine and we badly need to get a new cabin or house put up."

"That'll keep you busy, especially if you hope to do any mining."

Thomas laughed. "I'm trying to run two mines right now. It'd help if I knew what I was doing."

Frank nodded. "I heard about you and Sdzeè."

Thomas's eyes widened. "What have you heard?"

"Oh, the word about your partnership has made the rounds. I've heard some folks say you're taking advantage of a widow."

Thomas bristled. "That's ridiculous. She's the one that asked me to join in with her. I told her no but she insisted."

"Not saying I feel that way. Just telling you what's going around."

Thomas shook his head. "None of it's true."

"Anyway...how are things going? Getting a good start?"

"Actually that's why I'm here. We've got a boiler up and running at Sdzeè's and have a couple of steam points, but only piping to run one at a time. Any chance you'd have a bit of hose, a T-fitting and some couplings?"

Frank rubbed his chin for a second. "I think we might be able to help you out."

"I'll pay for the parts."

"We can worry about that later. Come on down to the mining shack and let's look around."

Frank opened the double doors of the shack and exposed a vast array of parts, pieces, chunks, and bits of equipment, hardware, and junk. He bent over and rummaged through a wooden crate labeled *DuPont*, which Thomas later realized once held dynamite.

"Ah," said Frank. "Here we go," he said as he pulled a T-connector from the box and handed it to Thomas. "And here," he said, handing Thomas a bunch of couplings and clamps.

He moved further into the dark shed and shoved more crates out of the way, coming up with a chunk of hose. "This long enough?"

Thomas moved in a bit further. "Yes, I think that'll do just fine."

Frank handed him the hose and slid past the crates, almost stumbling in the process. "I gotta get rid of some of this junk. See anything else you might need?"

Thomas looked around the shack. It was hard to really tell what all was in there, given the lack of light and the clutter. He noticed an iron wheel sticking up in the far corner. "What's that?" he said, pointing.

Frank squinted. "Oh that. An old steam hoist—the first one we used here. It's old and a bit noisy—still worked when we replaced it with the big double drum we have now."

Thomas caught himself nearly drooling. A hoist would make all the difference in hauling gravel to the surface. He pushed his way to the back corner to get a better look. It was old and rusty—a single-cylinder hoist, but it was love at first sight. "How much?"

"For the hoist? How about I lend it to you for sinking the shaft, and if you're happy with it afterward, you can give me a couple ounces of gold for it."

"Deal," said Thomas without hesitation.

"It's heavy. Probably ought to come up with your wagon and I'll get a couple of the boys to help load it. Your boiler big enough to run it?"

Thomas shrugged. "Not sure—I'm no mining engineer, something I've said more than once in the last couple days."

"It'll probably be fine. If not, shut down your steam points when you're hoisting. You're going to need a gin pole and a trip cable too."

Thomas stared at him as if he was speaking a foreign language.

Frank laughed and patted him on the shoulder. "Come on, bring your hose parts and I'll show you what I mean."

† † †

Thomas wiped his brow with the back of his hand. The early spring sun beat down on him and though it wasn't that warm, he worked up a sweat. What sounded simple according to Frank actually took much longer to get working. After fetching the hoist and a few other parts, Thomas and the others worked to get the gin pole set up and the dump bucket installed. This required several additional scavenging trips to other mines and no small amount of money.

Thomas took off his gloves and smacked them together to clear the dirt just as Declan sauntered up, cigarette dangling from his mouth.

"So, explain to me how all this is supposed to work."

Thomas shook his head, marveling at the man's lack of understanding. "Like I told you several times, after we thaw the gravel, we load the dump bucket. The steam hoist brings it to the surface, then travels along the cable and automatically dumps the gravel onto the pile."

"Hmm," said Declan. "Guess I'll have to see it in operation."

Thomas shook his head again, but Declan didn't notice—he'd already turned and headed back toward the shaft.

Even using the steam points, progress so far had been slow because they had to hand-carry the dirt a bucket at a time up the makeshift ladder. With the equipment in place, Thomas hoped they could get to bedrock, then connect with Sdzeè's old mine workings. *I just hope it's worth it*, thought Thomas, knowing that every day spent on Sdzeè's ground was one less on Angel Creek. He hoped once they could begin sluicing the winter dump that both mines could be worked, but that assumed they could get a full days work out of Declan. It also meant that Thomas would have to work with Sdzeè since John would have to keep a close eye on Declan in order to get anything out of him. *Can we send him back?* thought Thomas as he made his way to the shaft.

"Let's fire this thing up and move some dirt," said John, as he shoved another stick of wood in the boiler.

"You man the hoist and I'll muck out the hole and load the bucket," said Thomas as he climbed down into the shaft.

John nodded and watched Thomas descend. Once at the bottom, Thomas waved and John threw the lever on the hoist, lowering the dump bucket. There wasn't a lot of room in the shaft to maneuver, forcing Thomas to press against the wall just to have room to shovel into the bucket.

The bucket was about the size of a wheelbarrow, but

open on one end. It reminded Thomas of the Fresno scraper he used on the farm to excavate dirt. It took him a few minutes to shovel a load of thawed muck into the bucket. Digging the thick, heavy muck was a bit like shoveling molasses. Once you had a good bite with your shovel, moving it was tricky—as soon as you lifted the shovel, it flowed quickly off the sides.

Happy with the load, Thomas waved at John. "Take it away!"

John pulled the handle on the hoist and the bucket lurched upward. Thomas scampered out of the hole, all the while keeping an eye on its progress. It exited the hole, then traveled along the cable toward the gin pole. Thomas waited, fingers crossed, hoping the trip cable would work and the dirt would end up on the pile. "Keep ready to stop it in case things go south," he shouted at John over the noise of the hoist drum.

The bucket reached the trip mechanism, shuddered, then released, dumping the load of dirt.

"Works like a charm," said John as he reversed the hoist and brought the bucket back toward the shaft.

Declan stared at the pile of dirt, looked at the bucket traversing the cable toward the shaft, then peered at the hoist. "Oh, I see."

Thomas laughed and this time John shook his head.

"We'll have to reset the dump point once we start hoisting pay gravel instead of dirt," said Thomas.

John nodded and lowered the bucket into the shaft for the next round. "Your turn," he said to Declan, pointing at the ladder.

"Huh?"

"Get in the hole and load the bucket."

Declan grunted and flicked his cigarette, then proceeded down the ladder.

"How long you figure before we reach bedrock?" said John.

Thomas rubbed his chin. "Well, based on what Sdzeè told me, it could be twenty or thirty feet. Looks like we're at about twelve now."

John let out a low whistle.

"I know."

"Where is she anyway?"

"Sdzeè? I think she's down at the cabin."

"We should have told her to come watch the first go at it."

Thomas nodded. "She'll get to see a lot of it before we're done.

† † †

Declan jabbed the steam point harder but made no progress. After another week they were down over twenty feet. The material had changed from muck to gravel, a good sign, but they were still looking for bedrock.

"Something's wrong," yelled Declan.

Thomas looked down the hole, raised his hands, and shrugged. "What?"

"Can't go any further. Maybe something's broken," said Declan.

"I'm coming down."

Thomas reached the bottom of the shaft. It was tight quarters by design to keep the diameter just big enough to operate in, minimizing the amount of material to move.

"Let me try," he said, taking the point from Declan.

Thomas pulled the point from the hole and worked the valve. A burst of steam shot out, fogging the bottom of the hole. Satisfied the point was functioning, he worked it up and down through the gravel until he hit something solid. It felt different than bouncing off frozen ground or a boulder. "I think we've hit bedrock. Let's thaw all this layer and muck it out and see what we have."

Thomas signaled for the bucket and he and Declan began shoveling the thawed gravel. It wasn't long until angular pieces of bedrock appeared. Thomas continued scraping and shoveling until the floor of the shaft was cleared of gravel. At nearly twenty-seven feet, they had hit bedrock.

Thomas cupped his hands and yelled up the shaft "We're there!"

From the bottom of the shaft, Thomas could see John looking down, squinting into the dark hole. "What's that?" he shouted.

Thomas climbed into the bucket and gave John the thumbs up signal. A moment later the bucket lurched upward, headed to the surface. As it cleared the collar of the shaft, Thomas jumped off and let it continue on to the gravel dump.

"We hit bedrock."

"About time," said John.

"What is all the yelling about?" said Sdzeè.

Thomas turned to see her trotting up the path from the cabin. "I was about to fetch you and let you know. We've hit bedrock."

"That is wonderful news," she said. "Now what will you do?"

"We start drifting toward the creek, hoping to intersect the other mine workings. I just hope your husband was on bedrock as he drifted or we're going to miss it—or risk a cave in if we tunnel under."

"I think we need to rest for a spell since—what the...?"

The sound of whooping and hollering from the shaft stopped them short. They all peered over the edge to see Declan jumping up and down and carrying on. "I'm rich—I'm rich," he kept shouting.

Thomas threw the lever on the hoist and sent the bucket back down the shaft. When it reached the bottom he signaled for Declan to get in. Thomas reversed the winch and hoisted Declan to the surface. He hopped out of the bucket with a big grin on his face.

"What's all the yelling about?" said Thomas.

Declan unfolded his clenched fist to reveal a large gold nugget, about the size of a walnut and as thick as a nice slab of Sunday ham. The nugget was pitted and rough, but glimmered in the late afternoon sunlight. Thomas held out his hand, but Declan just stared at him.

"Let me see it," said Thomas.

Declan grudgingly handed it to him. Thomas was taken aback by the heft of it. He had seen nuggets other miners had found, but none this large. It was easily ten times bigger than any he and John found on Angel Creek.

Thomas turned it over and over in his hand, mesmerized by its glow. "How'd you find it?"

Declan held out his hand, but Thomas instead passed the nugget to John. Declan sighed. "It was under a bit of gravel along the back edge of the shaft, wedged in the bedrock. Had to pry around the rock with the shovel to free it."

"Nice, very nice," said John as he returned it to Thomas.

He took it, hefted it a couple more times, then handed it to Sdzeè. "Here, it's yours."

Declan glared. "What the h—"

"Got a problem?" said Thomas.

"You're darn right I do," said Declan, fists clenched.

"That's mine. I found it."

Thomas laughed, which only made Declan stiffen further. "You seem to forget who's claim we're on and who you work for. You're not a partner, you're an employee."

"You son of a—"

"Stop right there Declan," said John, stepping between them. "You better stand down now or you'll find yourself on the first stage out of here."

Declan glared long and hard, then a thin grin spread across his lips. He pulled his tobacco pouch from his vest and started rolling a cigarette, sealing the paper with a slow swipe of his tongue. Spitting at John's feet, he turned and walked away.

Standoff averted, Thomas shook his head. Declan walked past the cabin, flicking the used match into the tundra, then disappeared down over the hill.

"I swear, I want him gone or I'm liable to do something we'll all regret," said Thomas.

"He does seem to be an angry young man," said Sdzeè. "Do you think he is dangerous?"

"I don't think so," said John. "Thomas, if it were up to me he'd never even be here. The only reason I've put up with him thus far is for Stella's sake."

Thomas sighed and nodded. "Well, a couple of things are clear. One, if that nugget is any indication, this ground is incredibly rich, and two, Declan can't be trusted. If we turn our backs he's likely to rob all of us blind."

"Could it be just the excitement of the moment?" said Sdzeè.

"Possible," said John. "But I still think we need to keep an eye on him."

"Agreed," said Thomas. "Agreed."

† † †

CHAPTER 14

"How much further?" said John as he lowered the dump bucket down the shaft.

Thomas watched as the bucket descended with Declan holding the cable on the way down. Since their dust-up a week ago, things had settled down. Declan's attitude seemed to improve and he was actually putting effort into the work.

"Not sure," said Thomas. "Shouldn't be much longer before we intersect the other workings."

Once they hit bedrock, Thomas lined out the direction needed to drift in order to reach the workings now blocked by the caved shaft. They were running two steam points at a time and the thawing was going well. The further they got from the shaft, the longer it took to shuttle the thawed gravel to the bucket so it could be hoisted to the dump. Since the gravel on bedrock could be rich with gold, John had adjusted the trip mechanism to dump it before the rest of the pile, keeping it separate.

With a quick trip to town, Thomas procured a stack of 2x12 rough-cut planks. The process was thaw, shovel, scrape the bedrock, then level it out and put down the planks to run a wheelbarrow along. For the most part, the bedrock was fairly even, but in places it required them to use some gravel to level it out before placing the planks. Though Declan was better, Thomas occasionally had to prod him to keep moving. More than once he found him on his hands and knees, lantern close by his head, picking at the bedrock in hopes of another find.

Sdzeè had assured them that the old workings were right on bedrock. If this was the case, intersecting them would be no problem. Once opened up, Thomas hoped she would be temporarily satisfied with sluicing the dump gravels from her husband's work, as well as that produced during their current drifting effort. This would free him up to get back to work on Angel Creek, especially since there was a good bit of gravel to sluice from his winter work on the claim. So far, neither venture was paying for itself.

John shoved the winch handle over, stopping the empty bucket at the surface. "You sure you don't want me to go work in the hole for a while? I feel guilty sitting up here relaxing and watching the bucket go up and down."

"Somebody has to be the winchman," said Thomas. "Besides, there isn't a lot of extra room down there."

"If you want to swap jobs, I'm game. Sometimes I wonder what's going on down there with you and Declan out of sight."

"He's been better. Seems like he might have found a bit of work ethic laying around somewhere."

"Or maybe Stella talked to him," said John.

"Speaking of Stella, how do you think she and Emily are adjusting? Seems I don't spend much time with either of them with the long days we're putting in."

"I think Stella's doing fine—she's a rock. Emily, on the other hand, is miserable."

"I'm pretty sure she's still mad at me," said Thomas. "She seems so distant."

"The fact that you spend nearly eighteen hours day

away on Sdzeè's claim may have something to do with it."

Thomas hopped in the bucket and grabbed the cable. "I suppose you're right. We may have to make some changes, but I'm not sure how," he said as he disappeared into the shaft.

† † †

Declan jabbed the steam point into the face of the drift and began working it into the gravel. "We're going to need more steam hose before long," he said.

Thomas nodded in agreement as he pushed the other steam point deeper, working it back and forth as the gravel began to thaw. Progress was slower in the drift—to accommodate two people, its dimensions were larger than the shaft, which in turn meant more gravel to move. Some miners kept their drifts as small as possible, requiring them to walk completely stooped over. Thomas opted for larger workings, even though it meant more work. So far they were just digging a hole—not even sampling the gravel as they went to see if they were on a paystreak.

Declan pulled the steam point back a foot or so and then jabbed it forward to continue the thaw. Rather than meeting resistance, it plunged all the way to the hilt, causing Declan to lose his balance a smash his face against the gravel wall. He cursed.

"I think you've broken through," shouted Thomas.

Declan picked himself up, threw the valve on the point over and withdrew it from the hole. He looked into the two-inch opening but saw nothing. "Too dark."

"Let's work some more holes around it and see if we can open it up," said Thomas.

Excited by the prospect of finding the old drift, they quickened their pace. Soon two more holes broke through.

Thomas put down the steam point, grabbed a pick, then began swinging at the small area of thawed gravel. Slowly it fell away and before long, he had opened the hole to the point where they could take a look. Thomas grabbed up the lantern, held it through the hole, then pressed his face up close. Though he couldn't make out much, it was clear they had found the drift.

"Let's thaw enough so we can get in there," said Thomas.

They worked quickly, thawing and picking the gravel out of the way. Before long, the hole was large enough to crawl through. Thomas noticed that the floor of their drift was about two feet lower than the old. He took the lantern, told Declan to wait, and crawled through.

The lantern dimly illuminated the drift, and Thomas quickly noted that it was narrower and not as tall. He stooped over and looked in both directions. As planned they had intersected at nearly right angles, with the old workings running parallel to the creek just as Sdzeè had described. Thomas took a step to the left, the lantern dimmed and flickered, and he suddenly felt dizzy. The light went out and he stumbled, then fell, the lantern crashing to the ground. "Declan..."

Declan heard the crash, poked his head through the hole and saw Thomas laying on the floor of the drift. He crawled halfway through, grabbed Thomas by the feet, and dragged him back out of the old drift.

Thomas moaned, and rolled over, then sat up slowly. "What happened..."

"I don't know. You passed out or something."

"Help me to the shaft," said Thomas. "We need to get out of here."

On the surface, John helped Thomas out of the bucket and sat him down next to the shaft. He seemed okay, so he sent the bucket down again to hoist Declan out.

"What happened down there?" said John as Declan reached the top of the shaft.

"Not sure. He passed out or something after his lantern went out."

Thomas's voice was unsteady. "We broke through...to the old...drift."

"Great, but that doesn't explain why you passed out."

"Give me a minute," said Thomas, still drawing in deep breaths.

Declan rolled a cigarette, then offered it to Thomas. Thomas put his hand up, Declan shrugged and lit up.

Thomas's breathing settled. "I think I know what happened. The air is bad in there from being sealed up for so long. That's why my lantern went out right before I got dizzy."

"That makes sense," said John. "How long ago was the cave in?"

"Sdzeè said it was over two years ago."

"Now what?" said Declan. "We can't work down there without air."

"Maybe once we open it up more it will be fine," said John.

Thomas stood, his legs buckling at first, then stabilizing. "I don't know...maybe."

"You're now the winchman—at least for the rest of the day," said John. "We're going down and open it up more, but if our lanterns start to dim, we'll high-tail it out of there."

Declan grunted and tossed his cigarette on the ground. "Sounds delightful," he said, his face grim.

"I'm not sure you should," said Thomas.

"We'll be careful," said John. "Get on the winch unless you're not up to it."

"I can handle it. Just be careful down there and keep in touch," said Thomas as he lowered John into the mine.

Declan was just getting into the bucket for his turn when Sdzeè arrived from the cabin. "What is going on?"

Thomas explained to her they had broken through, and detailed the problem.

She placed her hand on his shoulder. "Are you fine now?"

"I'm okay. It was a bit scary. The worst thing is, I may now owe my life to yet another person."

Sdzeè laughed. "You seem to make a habit of needing rescue."

Thomas shook his head. "Yes, and now I owe Declan."

Sdzeè nodded. "How can I help?"

"Nothing you can do down there right now. I guess keep me company in case things go bad and you have to run for help."

Sdzeè sat down next to the hoist. Thomas stood, grasping the winch handle in case they needed a quick exit. For a long while, they heard nothing from down below. Thomas began to worry. The last thing he wanted to do was tell Stella and Emily that John wasn't coming back.

"I should go check on them. Do you think you can run the winch and bucket?"

Sdzeè stood and nodded. "I can."

Thomas climbed into the bucket and Sdzeè lowered him into the mine. Once at the bottom, he could hear the sound of the steam points working in the distance. Slowly he made his way through the dark until lantern light became visible. To his relief, both John and Declan were still vertical, working away at the opening.

"You boys okay?" he yelled above the sound of hissing steam.

Declan jumped, startled at his voice.

"Doing fine," said John. "Look," he said, pointing at the opening that was now three times the size of the hole Thomas crawled through.

"How's the air?"

"No problems so far, but we haven't gone in yet."

"Looks big enough for now," said Thomas. "Let's call it a day and leave it overnight. We'll check tomorrow."

"Sounds good," said John, noticing that Declan was already halfway to the shaft. "Anybody on the winch?"

"Sdzeè's running it for us—she's a natural."

With everyone on the surface, Thomas shut down the boiler. "Only one potential problem."

"What's that," said John.

"We can't cover the hole if we want to let air in, so hopefully we won't get too much thawing overnight."

"It has still been getting near freezing at night," said Sdzeè. "This is typical Alaska spring."

Thomas shrugged. "Hope so—we have to do it. Hopefully tomorrow we'll be able to get in there. If not, I don't know what we'll do."

† † †

The trip back to Angel Creek seemed longer than normal. It had been a long day and all were tired. Sdzeè offered to make dinner for the crew and even have them bunk there overnight, but Thomas knew that would lead to issues with Emily. Besides, Sdzeè didn't really have room and knowing her, she would give up the cabin for them and sleep in the tool shed.

The smell of fresh-baked something drifted through the air as Thomas pulled the wagon up to the cabin. *Stella's been busy again—must be tough guessing when to serve meals around here.* Already the sun was setting.

Thomas tied off the horse, leaving her hitched to the wagon as John and Declan jumped off and headed for the door. *I'll have to take care of her later—after dinner.*

He was the last in the door—into the cramped, nearly dark cabin. It took a moment for his eyes to adjust. Stella was busy at the stove, scooping something into bowls. John and Declan were already seated. Next to Declan sat Emily—hands folded on the table in front of her. Her face was a portrait of disdain. She stared at Thomas.

"Have a seat Thomas, we're ready to eat," said Stella, setting two steamy bowls of soup on the table.

Thomas hung his coat on the door hook and sat down. Two more bowls of soup arrived, along with a heaping plate of biscuits. Stella returned with a bowl and took a seat next to Emily. It was crowded around the table, but Emily didn't budge.

"You all must be tired," said Stella. "Everybody is so quiet."

"Sorry, dear," said John. "It has been a long day."

Emily huffed, then pushed the bowl away untouched.

"Not hungry?" said Thomas.

Emily crossed her arms and continued her silence.

Thomas shook his head and grabbed a biscuit, dipped it in the soup, and stuffed it in his mouth.

Stella stared down at her soup—Declan twirled his spoon with a half-grin on his face. Finally, John broke the silence.

"Come on Emily, what's the matter?"

Emily continued her long stare.

"Emily, I really wish—"

"I'm sick of it," she shouted. "Sick of this place, the cabin, the whole mess. And I'm especially sick of that ignorant Indian that's inserted herself into my life."

Stella gasped. John shot a glance at Emily. "Emily, that's—"

Thomas slammed his fist on the table, startling everyone. "That's enough. I won't have you talk about her that way. Whether you appreciate it or not, I owe her my life. Your petty jealousy has to stop—here and now."

Emily's hand shot up and covered her mouth. "Well, I never!"

Thomas glared at her. "You've changed."

John looked at Emily waiting for the tears to burst forth. They didn't come, rather a creature much like her mother emerged.

"No, you're the one that's changed," she blurted, face red, fists clenched. "You've ignored me and spent all your time with her. I demand you stay away from her and her ridiculous mine—I forbid you to see her again."

Thomas stared at her for a moment, eyes fixed, unaware of the others now watching in disbelief.

"Well?" she demanded, staring straight ahead. "What have you got to say?"

Thomas stood. "I've got a horse to take care of." He turned slowly, took his coat, and walked out the door.

Now the tears came, Emily holding her face in her hands. Declan, a hint of a grin on his face, put his arm around her. "There there, Emily. Everything will be fine."

John and Stella looked at each other, clearly not approving of Declan's move.

"I hate him! I hate him!" said Emily between sobs.

Declan pulled her just a bit closer, looked away from the others, and smiled.

† † †

Thomas rode slowly in the early morning darkness, allowing the horse to pick her way along the trail to Sdzeè's. He played the incident with Emily over and over in his mind. She was unhappy in the primitive conditions, being accustomed to more luxurious settings. *What had changed since Valdez?* he wondered. Certainly the conditions, but her jealousy was unexpected. After all, he had no designs on Sdzeè, apart from repaying the debt and fulfilling his promise to her.

The evening before was chilly in more ways than one. Thomas avoided the rest, turning in early and leaving before any of the others were awake. There was work to be done, yet he wanted to avoid talking about "it" as long as possible. No doubt John and Declan would arrive later with the wagon, but for now, he just wanted to think, to try and sort out what to do, or even how he felt about Emily.

Smoke was lazily rising from the chimney as Thomas approached Sdzeè's cabin. There was light emanating from the window casting a long shadow on the remnants of snow. He paused, unsure whether he should stop or continue up to the mine shaft and get busy. *No, better let her know I'm here.*

He tied up the horse to the hitching rail, and gently knocked on the door. There was a rustling sound inside, then the door opened, revealing Sdzeè in a nightdress down to her ankles, holding a .45-70 at ready.

"Whoa!" said Thomas. "Just me."

Sdzeè lowered the carbine. "What are you doing here

so early?" she said peering out the door and looking around. "Where are the others?"

"They'll be here later," said Thomas, hoping he was right.

"Have you eaten?"

"No, I left early before anyone was up."

"Well, come in," she said, grabbing him by the arm and pulling him gently into the one-room cabin. "I was about to make something to eat."

"I should just get busy."

"No, you need to eat. We have a busy day. Do not be silly."

Thomas closed the door behind him. The cabin was blistering warm compared to outside. He took off his coat and sat down.

"I must get dressed," said Sdzeè.

Thomas blushed a bit and stood up. "I'll leave."

"Do not be silly. Turn around and do not look."

Thomas turned and faced the door, his ears burning—unsure if it was the heat of the cabin or perhaps something else. There were rustling noises, then some quiet clattering from behind him. After a moment he felt a hand on his shoulder, which caused him to jump.

"You are jumpy," Sdzeè said.

Thomas turned slowly, not sure what to expect. She was standing there, fully dressed, a cup of steaming coffee in her right hand. "Here."

Thomas let out a sigh of relief, causing her to give him a quizzical look as he took the coffee.

"You are silly, Thomas. We are friends," she said, gently poking him in the arm. "Sit down," she ordered as she pulled a large cast iron skillet from the shelf and sat it on the stove. "Breakfast will be ready soon. Enjoy the coffee."

Now he felt stupid—stupid and embarrassed. He sipped the coffee as she worked, thinking about the night before. He could see how Emily would think there was something between him and Sdzeè, but as she said, they were friends. He owed her for saving his life, and despite Emily's feelings, he would honor that debt.

Sdzeè came to the table with two plates—bacon and eggs. "Eat."

"Where did you get the eggs?"

"I got them from Chicken," she said with a straight face, then burst into a giggle.

Thomas laughed. "Funny."

"There are some in town who have chickens. They give me a few eggs when I go down there," she said.

Thomas shoveled a bite, then chased it with a gulp of coffee. He was quite hungry and then realized why—he hadn't finished his dinner after the incident with Emily.

"You are very hungry, Thomas. Are they not feeding you well?"

Thomas put down his fork and debated. Should he tell her what happened? Knowing the jealousy toward her would no doubt change how she acted around Emily. *No, it was better for her to know.*

"It's not that," he began, then related the events of the night before to her. She listened intently, not interrupting. He finished and waited for Sdzeè to speak.

She smiled at him. "Thomas, I do love you. We are friends—good friends. But I do not want to cause a problem with you and Emily. It will be best for you to no longer work for me—to no longer come here."

Thomas shook his head. "No, I'll keep my promise to you. Emily will just have to get over it."

"Can you not see why it is hard for her?" said Sdzeè.

"Yes, but what concerns me more is how she has changed—or maybe I'm seeing the real her for the first time. Her mother turned out to be an evil woman, portraying an image of refinement, but being something else altogether."

"You think this runs in a family? That it could be passed on from mother to daughter?"

"No, that doesn't seem likely, but I am still concerned about the change in her."

"Do you still want to marry her?"

Thomas found the question a bit jarring. It was in the back of his mind for some time, but he didn't want to confront it. Perhaps the marriage was not meant to be—he pushed the thought back. "I don't want to think about it now—sorry."

"I understand. Sorry for asking. It is none of my business. Please, finish eating and then we will go up to the mine—if you are sure it is okay to continue."

"I'm sure," said Thomas.

CHAPTER 15

Thomas finished stoking the boiler, the fire flickering slowly as daylight filtered over the hills. It would be a bit of time before the steam-powered hoist was ready for service. Thomas was tempted to climb down the ladder and crawl through the opening to the old workings but decided against it. They would have to be careful, ensuring there was enough air seeping into the workings to prevent an episode like the last. Besides, he wasn't sure Sdzeè was strong enough to drag him back to safety should he pass out.

"I have filled all the lanterns," said Sdzeè as she returned from the cabin. "Shall we go down and look?"

"Well I'm itching to get down there, but I think we better wait for the boiler to get up to temperature," he said, not wanting to mention the real reason for waiting.

"Will John and Declan be here soon?"

"I don't know. Not sure what they'll think when they find I've gone already," said Thomas. *Pretty sure what Emily will think though.*

"Well, what should we do now?"

"Let's go down and fetch more wood for the boiler. The stack's getting a bit low."

Thomas grabbed the wheelbarrow and headed down the gentle hill, the iron wheel clattering over the mix of stones and tundra. Sdzeè ran ahead and beat him to the cabin.

"You are slow Thomas Thornton," she said, then laughed.

"Hey, it's early and your coffee is too weak to get me moving."

Sdzeè placed her hands on her hips. "Hmph," she said in mock disgust.

Thomas laughed at her as he grabbed an armful of firewood and dropped it into the wheelbarrow with a loud clang. Sdzeè pitched in and soon they had a heaping load. Thomas pushed it up the hill, Sdzeè following to pick up the stragglers that rolled off the wheelbarrow. They completed two loads and had nearly another loaded when they heard a wagon approaching—it was John and Declan. Thomas secretly hoped they were the only occupants.

"Mornin'," said John. "We wondered where you had gotten to."

"Yeah, what have you two been up to?" said Declan.

Thomas dropped the last of the wood onto the wheelbarrow. "We've been getting ready for a day's work and waiting for you stragglers to show up."

John laughed, but then turned serious. "Everyone was worried about you this morning."

"Everybody?" said Thomas, a look of doubt on his face.

"Well almost everybody," said Declan, who thought it was funny based on the laugh that followed.

Thomas scowled at him. "Let's just focus on the job at hand."

"Agreed, but we need to talk later," said John.

Thomas shrugged. Avoidance was much easier, but it was going to be a long, long summer unless things improved. *I'm not sure what to think*, he thought as he pushed the wheelbarrow to the boiler.

John arrived right behind him after securing the horse and wagon at the cabin. "I see you've got the boiler up and going. Are we ready to go down and take a look?"

Thomas glanced at the pressure gauge. "Looks like she's ready to work. Let's go down and have a look. Declan, grab that coil of rope—we're going to need it."

"What for?"

"You'll see when we get to the opening," said Thomas. "Sdzeè, will you operate the winch for us? I want John to go down with us."

Sdzeè nodded and took up her position at the handles. "Ready when you are."

It took two trips for the three to descend the shaft—Thomas and John in one trip, Declan and the rest of the equipment in the other. Lanterns lit and at the ready, they made their way to the opening into the old workings. Thomas poked his head through and held the lantern in as far as he could. The flame flickered ever so slightly but continued to burn.

"Looks like we might have enough air now," he said. Thomas took one end of the rope and tied it around his left ankle, making sure to double-knot it.

"Ah, I see your plan," said John. "Kinda like the high priest in the Bible."

Declan looked at him and shrugged, not catching the analogy.

"Well, I'm not holy, but if I get struck down in there you two can drag me out. One of you needs to keep an eye on me. I want to get to both ends to check out the conditions."

"I'll watch," said John, which, for some reason, was a comfort to Thomas.

Thomas sat the lantern on the floor of the old work-ings and crawled up and into the narrow space. He paused and took a big breath. The air was stale but breathable. "Good so far," he said, turning to the right. "I'm going to head upstream first and get a look at the face."

"Be careful and don't hesitate to have us yank you out at the slightest hint of bad air," said John.

"Don't worry, I don't want a repeat of yesterday," said Thomas as he continued, stooped over with lantern in hand. He counted his steps to get an idea of the length of the drift, pausing frequently to make sure he could breathe. The lantern flame held steady, which provided some measure of reassurance. The rope somewhat hin-dered his movement and he had to half-kick to get slack for the next step. Thirty paces later, he could see the end of the drift. Lifting the lantern as high as possible, he surveyed a moment frozen in time.

The remains of a fire were crammed up against the face, mostly charcoal, but with some wood remaining. A metal wheelbarrow, painted orange, lay near the burnt wood, tipped on its side. A pick and shovel leaned up against the left wall near the face. A small metal bucket, dinged and dented, sat next to them. Thomas reflected on what he saw—this was the last work of a dead man. He suddenly had a wave of adrenaline sweep from his chest to his head. Sdzeè's husband was trapped somewhere in here.

"How's it going?" echoed John's voice from the open-ing.

"I'm at the face. There's some equipment here and the remnants of William's last thaw fire," said Thomas as he grabbed the pick. "I'm going to take a swing at the gravel, then head back your way," he yelled.

Thomas swung the pick and was met with a solid

clang of metal against frozen gravel. No reason to expect anything else—it was more out of curiosity than expectation. He held the lantern close, hoping to see the telltale glitter of gold. He found none. Leaning the pick against the wall, he turned and made his way back to the opening, pausing for a moment.

"How's the air?" said John, he and Declan looking through the hole.

"Not too bad. A bit stale is all. We might need to think about how to get some ventilation going. I'm not sure there's enough air circulation for us to work down here. We'll have to see."

"Maybe Frank can help us out," said John. "Might be worth a trip over there."

Thomas nodded, then continued along the drift in the direction of the caved shaft. He made his way slowly, lantern held high so as not to trip or run into anything unexpected. The floor of the drift was uneven, but not so much so that you couldn't push a wheelbarrow full of gravel along it. It looked to him as though William hadn't excavated very deep into the bedrock—in some places not at all. *Probably missed a lot of gold*, thought Thomas.

Thomas counted the paces. He knew the new shaft was roughly twenty feet upstream from the original. He walked slowly, tugging the rope with his left foot. The lantern grew a little dimmer but didn't go out. He wasn't sure how long he could spend in the drift but pressed on. At about ten paces he saw the end—a jumbled pile of cribbing, muck, and gravel, slumping into the drift. It was a massive cave-in, brought about by thawing of the muck near the surface. Thomas inched closer, aware that the back could be unstable, but hoping it was now frozen solid.

He reached the jumbled pile of wood and muck. Kicking it confirmed it was frozen. Some of the cribbing was loose, however, as were portions of a crude ladder made from spruce poles. He continued to survey the area, adjusting the dim lantern as he looked. Moving it over a section of splintered ladder, he caught a glint of something beneath it, partially hidden. Thomas pulled at the remnants of the ladder and part of it yielded, cracking and breaking free. He bent over and moved the lantern close, hoping to find a gold nugget in the debris.

He got on his hands and knees, pushed his head between the splintered ladder and saw it. It was gold—a gold wedding band on a frozen finger—it was William.

† † †

Thomas half-rolled through the opening, landing between John and Declan. He gasped for breath, chest heaving.

"Air's bad? Why didn't you have us haul you out?" said John as he worked to untie the rope from Thomas's ankle.

"It's not that," said Thomas between gasps.

"What then?" said Declan impatiently.

"I found him—I found Sdzeè's husband."

"Where?" said John.

"At the bottom of the shaft in a frozen jumble of wood and muck."

"So he's just laying there?" said John.

"No, the only thing exposed is one hand. I saw a glint of gold and it turned out to be his wedding band."

"My word," said John. "Now what?"

"Sdzeè will be devastated," said Thomas. "It's going to be real difficult to recover the body."

"We could use the steam points to get him out," said Declan.

"Yes, we could, but we run the risk of cooking him," said Thomas, realizing he could have chosen better words.

"I think we have two choices," said John. "Either we thaw the gravel and run the risk, or we seal off the drift in that direction and consider him buried."

Thomas stood, brushed himself off, and picked up the lantern. "I've got to tell Sdzeè."

"Do you want me to do it?" said John.

"No, I'll do it, but I'd like to do it privately. Can you stay down here for a bit?"

Declan grunted. "Sure," said John.

"It won't take long. We'll let her decide what to do," said Thomas.

Thomas made his way back to the bucket, his gut churning. *This isn't going to be easy.* He signaled for Sdzeè to bring him up, a trip that seemed too short for the task at hand. He reached the surface and hopped out.

"How are things down there?" she asked.

Thomas made his way over to her next to the winch, his face grim.

"Where are the others? Why are you so quiet. Did something happen?"

"Sdzeè, I have something to tell you."

"Please. You are making me very nervous. Did someone get hurt?"

"Here, sit," said Thomas, taking her hand and guiding her to the log bench a short distance from the shaft. She sat down, staring into his eyes. Thomas noticed her hands were trembling. *Did she know?*

"Please tell me now."

Thomas could delay no longer. "Sdzeè, I surveyed

the old workings in both directions. At the old shaft, I found something. I found William."

She stared at him for a moment, no sign of emotion. She turned and looked at the winch, then back to Thomas. "William?"

"Yes, I'm so sorry."

The news registered. She covered her face with her hands and began to sob quietly. Thomas moved closer and put his arm around her shoulder, unsure how to comfort her. He realized how hard it must have been for her—to walk by the caved shaft each day as they worked, knowing that he was still down there—wondering if he suffered.

Sdzeè wiped the tears with her sleeve, regaining her composure. "We must give him a decent burial," she said.

Thomas dreaded telling her the options but had no choice. "I know, but it will be hard. He is mostly buried in the cave in. It will be very hard to thaw and get him out."

"What else can we do? We must try."

Thomas hesitated, then offered the alternative. "We could bury him where he lays, seal off that end of the drift, and erect a memorial to him both underground and at the surface."

Sdzeè looked down, then leaned forward, head in her hands. Thomas was at a loss for words—at least any that would be of comfort. After an awkward silence that seemed to last forever, Thomas spoke. "We'll do whatever you want. It's completely up to you."

She looked up at him and smiled ever so slightly, cheeks still stained with tears of grief. "I thought I was over it—the accident. It has been two years, but now I still grieve. Is it dangerous? To recover him for burial?"

Thomas thought revealing the potential horror of recovering the body using steam points wasn't something she needed to hear. "It could be dangerous if the shaft slumps once we start thawing," he said, something actually within the realm of possibility.

"I want to see him."

"Sdzeè, very little of him can be seen. Only his hand is exposed."

"So he is already buried—though not properly? What do you think we should do, Thomas?"

"As you say, for all intents and purposes, he is buried. We can complete it and seal it off as I said. It will give you a place where you know he is at rest. It is the safest thing to do."

She sighed. "You are right. There is no purpose in digging him up only to bury him in another place. I just want it to be a place of rest, not exposed and looked at every day."

"We can do that, Sdzeè, I promise."

They stood and she hugged him, tears flowing again. Thomas embraced her lightly, uncomfortable, but glad there was no one to see. She needed him now—a friend.

† † †

"Seems stupid to do this," said Declan as he dragged one more plank down the old drift.

Thomas took the plank and gave him a look. "I told Sdzeè we'd seal this end up in respect of her husband. Doesn't much matter what you think."

Declan grunted and trudged back towards the opening to fetch another.

Thomas was successful in convincing Sdzeè not to come into the old workings. They spent a better part of the morning sealing off the drift. Thomas had built a log frame on the sides, then notched in a cross piece for the top. It took a bit of work to excavate the sides enough to get a tight fit. With a final log wedged across the bottom, they worked at boarding up the rest of it using rough-cut planks. Only a few more and it would be complete, despite the foot-dragging and complaining by Declan.

John and Declan arrived with the last two planks. Thomas nailed them up, then stepped back to observe the result. "Looks good," he said.

"Yes, it's a good fit. Shall we write his name and dates on it?" said John.

"I told Sdzeè we would. It will have to wait until we get some white paint. I need to make a cross for the surface location as well."

"How's she doing?" said John.

"As well as expected. It opens old wounds of course."

After the news of the find, Sdzeè returned to her cabin and Thomas didn't follow. He had no idea what she was doing, but more than likely needed time alone. *I'll check on her later.*

"Can we get back to finding some gold now?" said Declan as they exited the old drift.

"You're a compassionate git, aren't you," said John, shaking his head.

Thomas gave Declan a look—a long stare, then said "Get your steam point and get things set up at the face of the drift. You'll need to clean up the remains of the fire and get William's tools out of your way. Then get to thawing. John can work on ramping the entrance to the old drift to make it easier to move the thawed gravel to the shaft."

"What are you going to do?" said Declan.

"I've got an errand in town."

† † †

Thomas returned in the late afternoon, stopping at Sdzeè's cabin. He tied off the horse, then gently knocked on the door, not knowing what to expect. There was no answer. He knocked louder with the same result. *Maybe she's up at the mine.*

As Thomas neared the shaft, he could see Sdzeè sitting on the bench in the sun. She looked up as he approached.

"Hello, Thomas. Where have you been?"

"I had to go to town and pick up a couple things."

"Oh?"

"I managed to scare up some white paint for William's markers, and I have something for you." Reaching into his pocket, he pulled out something wrapped in paper. He handed it to her.

Sdzeè slowly unwrapped it, revealing a gold chain. She held it up. Attached to it was a gold wedding band. A single tear rolled down her left cheek. "Where?—how?"

"Here, let me help you," said Thomas as he took the chain.

Sdzeè pulled her long black hair aside, and Thomas fixed the clasp. She smiled. "Where did you ever find a chain?"

"Well, it took a bit of searching, but I finally found someone in Chicken willing to sell me one."

Sdzeè lifted the ring and looked at it for a moment. "Thank you again, Thomas Thornton."

"You're welcome. Now you have something to remember him by. I hope it wasn't too forward of me, but I thought you would like it as a keepsake."

"It is fine. I am happy you gave it to me."

Thomas smiled, trying to put out of his mind the gruesome task of removing the ring from William's frozen finger. Fortunately, Sdzeè hadn't seen his remains. It was better for her last memory to be one of the living, not the dead.

"I better get down there and check on things. Are you the winch operator today?" said Thomas.

"Yes, I have been helping, running the winch and keeping the boiler stoked. They have been down there a long while."

"Okay, send me down," said Thomas.

Sdzeè raised the bucket, then lowered Thomas to the bottom of the shaft. Thomas could hear the steam points hissing—a good sign. He reached John first, admiring the ramp and improvements to the opening into the old workings.

"Looks good," said Thomas as John closed the valve on the steam point.

"Yeah, I figure we should probably put down planks to make wheeling gravel to the shaft easier, especially in the old section since it's so rough and uneven."

"I agree. We have two wheelbarrows now so we should be able to muck things out much quicker after a thaw," said Thomas.

John looked down, then glanced back toward the shaft. "I hate to ask, Thomas, but how far are we going to take this?"

Thomas knew what he meant. Nearly a month into the mining season and no work on their claim. Soon their stockpile would be thawed and it would be time to sluice. "I know what you mean, but we should probably wait a day or two before we bring it up to Sdzeè."

"Right," said John.

"Let's push the drift forward a few days and get some gravel on the stockpile, then we can broach the subject with her. I want to pan as we go to see if it's worth doing more than that," said Thomas. "Finding one big nugget could just be an anomaly."

"Maybe hold off on planking the whole thing until we see," said John.

Thomas nodded and headed down the drift toward Declan who was busy ramming the steam point into the face, sometimes with a bit too much vigor. "How's it going?" Thomas yelled.

Declan turned off the steam point and dropped it on the ground. Thomas shook his head. *We'll be lucky if our equipment survives him.*

"Going okay I guess. I was about ready to start swinging the pick and busting this stuff up, but now that you're here it's your turn," said Declan, that familiar twisted grin spreading across his face.

"That's not what we're paying you for, but let's get to it," said Thomas, avoiding the conflict and grabbing a pick. "Let's get this mucked out and see what we've got. Hopefully we'll find some gold."

Thomas swung the pick and the gravel slumped from the face. How much does one owe for their life he wondered. They had spent a lot of time, a lot of time away from Angel Creek. It would be tough to call it quits here and Sdzeè would be disappointed. With each shovel load into the wheelbarrow, he hoped they would find gold. *If not, it's all been for naught.*

† † †

CHAPTER 16

Thomas swirled the pan gently, tipping it to wash away the remaining black sand. So far the results from Sdzeè's mine were disappointing. Over the last several days, they extended the drift another twenty feet. With each round of thawing, Thomas took multiple samples, both from the gravel and the weathered bedrock on the floor of the drift. It wasn't the expected windfall, but rather a little color here and there—nothing approaching the nugget Declan found. He thought perhaps they should expand their efforts near the base of the shaft where the nugget was found. That meant a big change in plans and a lot more work. He pushed the thought aside for now.

Swirling the last bit of black sand away revealed a band of gold, the most Thomas had seen in a single pan since last year. *This looks better,* he thought as he picked through the flecks of gold. The noise of the creek drowned out the sound of approaching footsteps.

"Nice!" said Declan, startling Thomas and almost making him spill the entire contents of the gold pan.

"Don't sneak up on me like that. I could have shot you."

Declan laughed. "With what? You're not carrying a gun."

"Yeah, I'm not like you with your sidearm. I don't know how you manage to wear that thing all day," said

Thomas.

Declan just laughed. "Never know when trouble might crop up. So, looks like we're in the gold now, huh?"

"Yes, but still not as much as I'd like to see. We'll go ahead and spend a little more time stockpiling—maybe push the drift ahead another fifteen or twenty feet."

"Oh joy," said Declan. "I can't wait to get back in that cramped hole."

Thomas shook his head and handed the pan to Declan. "Here, a bonus for you."

Declan took the pan and swirled it as Thomas headed up from the creek to the shaft, leaving him to stare at the glittering flakes.

Sdzeè was sitting on the bench, waiting to winch John out of the mine when he was ready. "How was the pan?"

Thomas shrugged. "Better, but nothing that will make us rich unless there's a lot of material. But I think it's worth expanding the face and driving forward another fifteen feet to get some more gravel to sluice."

"What then?"

Thomas had procrastinated telling Sdzeè about the discussion with John—the need to get back to working on their own claim. Since he and Sdzeè never discussed the details of their arrangement, it was open-ended. Now he felt he could wait no longer.

"Sdzeè, we have to talk about where we go from here. I know I promised to work for you, and we have accomplished a lot. We will have stockpiled a fair amount of gravel in another few days—but, John and I also have to consider our claim."

Sdzeè looked at him and smiled. "You have done much, Thomas Thornton. I release you from your obligation."

"I'm not looking to be released, just time to work on our own claim. Once we are set up and running we can divide the labor and sluice gravel on both claims."

"That is fair," she said. "Go and work on your claim."

"No, we're going to push your drift a little further and get enough gravel to process along with what William and you stockpiled. Then we will work on Angel Creek."

"That is a good plan, Thomas. And it will make Emily happy."

Thomas pulled the pouch from his pocket and slowly rolled a cigarette. *Will anything make Emily happy?*

† † †

Three days later, they had advanced the drift eighteen feet. The crew spent long days thawing, shoveling, and winching the pay gravels to the surface. Thomas and John conferred and decided it was enough. The sluice boxes on Sdzeè's claim appeared serviceable, even though they had been idle since her husband's death. They would have to check them out thoroughly when the time came. Once things were up and running on Angel Creek, they'd come back and set up the sluices.

The biggest issue was how to divide the labor. Declan couldn't be trusted to work without oversight, so either John or Thomas would have to supervise. This meant the women would have to help with sluicing if they hoped to make any real progress. Thomas knew two would be willing, the third—well she would likely not.

Thomas shut down the boiler, releasing the pressure. They had no further need of it now—at least until they decided to expand the drift. With the amount of work already before them, Thomas doubted they'd be doing any more thawing at Sdzeè's in the near future.

"Thank you, Thomas, for all the hard work—and you too John," said Sdzeè.

"You're welcome," said John.

"Tomorrow we start on Angel Creek," said Thomas. "Getting those thaw fires going and hoisting gravel."

"No, you are wrong, Thomas," said Sdzeè.

Thomas looked at her quizzically. "What are you talking about?"

"You will take all the equipment here to your claim. It makes no sense for you to thaw with wood fire when all this is here," she said.

Thomas hadn't thought of it, though it was a great idea. "I guess I've been so focused on finishing here and getting back to the routine on Angel Creek I wasn't thinking very clearly."

She smiled. "You are welcome to it. There is no need to thaw more here this year."

"Thank you, Sdzeè. This is going to make things a lot easier for us. Going to take some work to dismantle and move everything, then set it back up," said John.

"Yes," said Thomas. "But it will be worth it in the long run."

Declan arrived from playing around with a gold pan down at the creek. "What's going on?"

Thomas and John explained the plan to him.

"Great. That's going to be a lot of work," said Declan, throwing the pan on the ground with a clatter.

"Agreed," said Thomas. "Tell you what, why don't we all take a day off tomorrow to rest a bit before we dive into the move. We've been pushing pretty hard."

"That sounds like a good idea," said Sdzeè. The others agreed and it was settled—tomorrow would be a free day.

† † †

Declan reached the head of the valley and sat down on a large rock. He took out a handkerchief and wiped his forehead. Though sunny, the spring air wasn't very warm, but the climb was enough to work up a sweat. He laid the Winchester Model 1873 carbine across his knees and looked around. He was somewhat amazed that John let him borrow the rifle—he didn't even ask Thomas as he was pretty sure of the answer. John only agreed after a bit of cajoling and promising to bring back some fresh meat to camp.

Caribou migrated through the area each spring, and though fresh meat would be nice, Declan really just wanted to get away from the rest of them—knowing if he stuck around, Thornton would come up with some menial chore that would consume most of the day. He was content to sit on the rock in the sun all day. Rolling a cigarette, he lit up and surveyed the next valley that lay before him.

It was typical of those in the Fortymile—rolling hills with sparse trees at higher elevations and mixed stands of spruce, birch, and poplar in the lowlands. The valley appeared to be deserted, with no sign of human activity. The creek that flowed in the lowlands was pristine. To Declan's untrained eye it looked as though it had never been mined. Though he cared little for history, no doubt the swarm of humanity that followed the gold rush had been here—had prospected the creek and, judging from the look of it, found nothing. Declan thought of prospecting it himself, but his lack of ambition brought him to his senses.

Nothing moved in the valley below—no sign of caribou or other game. *Just as well*, thought Declan. Downing an animal meant more work—skinning, quartering, and packing. It was easier to enjoy the spreading warmth of spring sun on his day off.

Flicking his third cigarette to the ground, he noticed something among the dissolving shadows in the valley. He strained to get a better view, then stood. He couldn't be sure, but it looked like some sort of structure, its lines out of place among the natural surroundings. His curiosity overcoming his inertia, he started down the valley.

It was definitely a structure—a building. He covered over half the distance, then turned and looked back up the valley, realizing how much elevation he'd have to gain to return. He paused, then decided to push forward. *Who knows, maybe there's something of value down there.*

Nearing the structure he saw what it was—an old, dilapidated cabin. The door was hanging by one hinge, partially open. On one side of the door, traps, rusted and red, hung from a spike. *A trappers cabin.* The roof sagged from years of neglect and heavy snow. Declan approached and tugged on the door. It swung open the rest of the way, revealing the dark interior. Hoping it wasn't about to collapse, he ducked down and entered.

A musty smell greeted him. Slowly his eyes adjusted to the dark. The builder had excavated the floor down almost two feet to save on the number of logs needed during construction. This, along with the dirt floor, added to the bleakness of the place. Declan looked around—a single bunk with rotting bedding, a crude table with a tin cup and plate, the remnants of some uneaten meal, and a rusting wood stove completed the decor.

It was hard to tell if the trapper had moved on, or left in a hurry and never returned. Declan rummaged through the cabin, slinging things around as he searched for something of value. *Not even a mangy pelt*, he thought as he exited. He looked around the outside, finding nothing but the remnants of a few stretching boards for pelts.

It was clear the cabin had been deserted for a long, long time. He pushed the door closed, took one last look, and headed back up the valley. *I wonder who else knows about this...*

Finally reaching the rock at the divide of the two valleys, Declan sat down on the ground, the large rock at his back. It wasn't a steep climb, but long enough to require a break. He lit up a cigarette and rested against the rock. He daydreamed, thankful to not be in a cramped, dark, frozen hole picking at gravel. He reached into his pocket for the tobacco pouch and rolled another cigarette. After several puffs, he spotted movement in the valley below, just beyond the cabin. At first, it was just glimpses of white moving between the trees. He clutched the carbine, not sure what to expect. The white apparitions emerged from the trees and moved casually into the open—caribou.

Declan watched as they moved slowly up the valley toward him, feeding on lichens as they went. He counted at least thirty. He snuffed out the cigarette and slumped down further, pulling his hat low to hide his face. The caribou continued feeding up the valley. Ten minutes later they were a mere fifty yards from him on the left. He slowly raised the carbine, took aim at the closest cow, and fired. She went down, then jumped up and started to run. Declan leaped to his feet, racked the action on the carbine and chose another. He continued firing until the click told him the rifle was empty. He reached into his pocket, grabbed more rounds, and quickly shucked them into the rifle.

By this time there were three caribou down, each struggling to get up. The rest of the herd had turned and was headed down the valley at a fast clip. He fired into the group until the rifle was empty, not bothering to see if any fell. He reloaded again, but realized it was pointless—the herd was now a good two hundred yards away on a dead run.

He walked over to the nearest caribou and poked its rump with the rifle barrel. It was dead. He moved on to the other two, both lying within a few feet of each other and struggling to get on their feet. One was shot through the hindquarter, the other had been hit high in the middle of its back, breaking the spine. Declan looked at them, smiled, then turned his attention down the valley. He could see two others down, both wounded. He raised the rifle, aimed at the nearest, and paused. He lowered the rifle. If he returned with half a box of shells gone and nothing to show for it, there'd be an inquisition. John warned him before he left not to waste ammunition since it wasn't easy to obtain.

He looked at the caribou, struggling to stand, legs flailing and blood spreading over the ground. He pulled the Colt Frontier revolver from the holster, then paused, and replaced it. He turned and started up the hill, the anguished sounds of dying creatures fading as he topped the divide and began the long walk home.

† † †

John greeted Declan as he returned to camp in the early afternoon. "Have any luck?"

Declan shook his head and handed the rifle and shells to John. John looked at the half-empty box and then back at Declan.

"Looks like you did some shooting," he said. "I told you not to waste ammunition."

Declan shuffled his feet and looked at the ground to hide the smirk on his face. He regained composure. "I'm really sorry John, I guess I'm just a lousy shot."

"What happened?"

"Well I was far up the valley and I saw a single caribou standing there. I thought it was pretty close so I started shooting, but it just stood there. My last shot hit the ground at its feet and it took off."

John shook his head. "How far away was it?"

"Well, I paced it off afterwards and it was 300 paces," said Declan, pulling a number out of the air.

"That's over 250 yards. If you knew anything about guns, you'd know that's a really long shot with this rifle."

"Well I guess I found that out, didn't I?"

"Guess so. Too bad it took half a box for you to figure it out."

"I'll do better next time," said Declan.

If there is a next time, thought John.

Thomas emerged from the men's dormitory. "Any luck?" he called as he joined them.

"Nope," said Declan. "I tried though."

"It's a sad story, Thomas. One that cost a half box of shells," said John.

Thomas got the drift. "I hope everyone's going to be well-rested for tomorrow. We've got to dismantle the boiler and hoist assembly for transport here. I figure it's going to take a number of trips to get everything moved."

"And then it's going to take a lot of time to get things set up here," said John. "Probably be a week before we can actually get to thawing gravel."

"Right. Plus we need to set up a gin pole at the dump and get the trip cable installed," said Thomas. "It will be worth it in the long run."

Declan lit up another cigarette. "Seems like a lot to me. Too much work."

Thomas gave him a sour look. "Well, the alternative

is you build a fire each day, thaw the gravel overnight, cleanup the charcoal and ashes, break up the thawed gravel, hand-carry it to the shaft, hoist it by hand, and carry it to the dump."

"That doesn't sound very appealing opposed to thawing with steam points and hoisting with machinery," said John.

"I guess so," said Declan grudgingly.

Thomas couldn't believe the height of laziness in Declan. He waffled from being somewhat diligent to completely slothful. Clearly he was raised with no work ethic. He was like a stubborn ox that wouldn't plow without constant urging. More and more, the prospect of having him do anything without direct supervision seemed impossible. *I wish there was some way to motivate him,* thought Thomas, knowing full well the adage of teaching an old dog new tricks likely applied.

"We'll hit it hard tomorrow and it will be fun," said Thomas.

"Fun," said Declan. "I can't wait."

† † †

CHAPTER 17

It took the better part of a week to dismantle and move the equipment from Sdzeè's and set it up at Angel Creek. The hardest part was setting up the gin pole and trip cable assembly. With the ground frozen, they had to get the boiler running in order to thaw the ground for the pole. Once that was set and tamped firmly in place, guy wires were added to it. Thomas gave Declan the job of moving some large boulders to the base of the pole to stabilize it. The hoist headframe was finally in place and everything was set and ready to go.

It was early morning when Thomas fired up the boiler, still waiting for Declan and John to arrive. Stella had cooked up a magnificent breakfast for them to celebrate the start of the operation—pancakes, fried potatoes, and bacon—lots of bacon. Thomas was the first to leave the cabin, the chill he got from Emily was colder than the morning air. They had said little since the contentious incident in the cabin. Thomas kept expecting it, but his future father-in-law remained silent about it as well. The only person that seemed to be enjoying the tension was Declan. Thomas only hoped he would carry his weight. Work was going to get a lot more intense as they started sluicing along with thawing and stockpiling.

John arrived, Declan straggling behind. Thomas had the boiler up to pressure and already cycled the hoist twice to make sure everything was in order. "We're ready to move some gravel," he said.

Declan rubbed his hands together. "Oh joy."

John gave him a hard look. "Can you dispense with the attitude for once?"

Declan widened his eyes. "Who me? Whatever do you mean."

"And get rid of the sarcasm as well," said John. "The only reason you're here is that Stella felt obligated. I can send you packing in a heartbeat and I'm sure Thomas won't mind a bit."

"You think Stella will let you get away with that?" said Declan.

"Don't be so confident. I've already discussed it with her and she agrees. If you act up, you're history—and on your own nickel too."

Declan shrugged. "Okay. I'll do better."

"That's all we ask," said Thomas, hoping he was sincere.

† † †

Thomas dumped the last load of the day onto the new pile and yanked the hoist into neutral. Since the winter stockpile was still largely frozen, they opted to start a new dump with the thawed material, allowing them to begin sluicing sooner. The rate of thawing and hoisting was not enough to keep up with a sluicing operation, so John and Thomas decided to spend another week stockpiling material.

Sdzeè came around a couple of times but didn't stay long. Emily avoided her but made sure everyone knew how she felt about it. Tensions were still running high, and rather than resolve it, Thomas threw himself into the work, spending twelve to sixteen hours a day thawing and hoisting gravel. He realized at some point he would have to face the issue, especially since, as far as he knew, they were still engaged.

Engaged. He wasn't sure how he felt about that now. In her element in Seattle, Emily was a prim and proper lady—at least what Thomas saw fit that description. Out of her element in the far north, the other side of her personality emerged. Thomas thought back to advice his mother gave him years ago. *"Thomas, when you find the one you are sure is your soulmate, spend a year before you marry."* It made sense to him now. Through good and bad, a person's true personality will eventually be revealed. Right now, he didn't like what he was seeing.

So much like Lydia her mother. Her secret life had been a great distress to John and Emily, yet he could see glimpses of her in Emily. Of greater concern was where John's loyalties lay. *No doubt he'll stand by his daughter.*

He thought about ending it, but that would place him at odds with John and jeopardize his relationship with Stella. *Maybe it's just a phase—or maybe simple jealousy.* There was no reason for her to be jealous. He had done nothing to warrant Emily's disdain—no hatred, towards Sdzeè. Sure he spent a lot of time over there, but it was work—and he wasn't going there alone. Maybe she deserved another chance. He needed advice, and Stella was the only one he trusted to have a clear head.

"Wake up you dreamer," shouted John.

Thomas snapped back to attention, realizing he'd been standing there with his hand on the idled hoist handle for who knows how long. "I'm awake he said," dropping his hand quickly.

"Dinner's on and Stella won't be happy if she has to serve it in shifts," said John.

"I'll be right there," said Thomas, wondering how he could get Stella alone to talk. It wouldn't be easy with everyone crammed into the small cabin.

† † †

Dinner conversation centered around the work of the day and what tomorrow would hold. Thomas's attempts at engaging Emily were largely ignored—met with cold indifference. Thomas was unaware of Emily's previous outburst—the one where she vehemently said she hated him. She was playing a game, trying to maintain the upper hand without consideration of what might be lost. To the others, it was nerve-wracking, save for Declan.

Dinner finished to the relief of nearly everyone. "I'm going to go make sure we have enough wood for the boiler for tomorrow," said John.

"I'll help," said Thomas, standing and relieved for an out.

"No, you've been working too hard. Sit."

Thomas sat back down as Stella cleared the table. She worked hard and Thomas knew this wasn't what she expected when she married and came north. But she always stepped up, no matter the task or challenge.

"Declan, I need water for dishes," said Stella.

Declan sighed. "Again?"

"Yes, every day," she said.

Declan stood up, took the bucket from her, then said, "Hey Em, you want to help me?"

Thomas furrowed his brow and Emily noticed. "Sure," she said. "It's too crowded in here anyway."

Declan smiled and opened the door for her. "After you milady."

Thomas thought he was going to be sick. "You okay?" said Stella.

He didn't know where to begin. "What's with that cutesy nickname—Em?"

"That's something new," said Stella. "I don't know if you've noticed, but they've been playing cat and mouse for quite a while."

He had noticed. "I assume that's for my benefit?"

"Maybe on her part, but I think Declan has designs on her."

Thomas's fists tightened. *I knew he was trouble from day one.* He blew out a long breath, relaxed, and leaned back in the chair. "I'm glad we're alone for a minute, I need your advice. What should I do about Emily?"

"What do you mean? About her and Declan?"

"Well that, but more about my engagement. I'm starting to question if I really know her at all."

"Are you thinking about breaking it off?"

"I don't know what to do. She has been so different, so angry."

"Well she isn't happy here I'm afraid. She has nothing to do besides helping me, and actually it's nothing I can't handle. She ends up doing little or nothing all day—just sitting around and fussing about, well frankly, everything."

"But why, how can she change so much?"

"I hesitate to say this, but she is used to attention—a lot of it. And with you and John gone every day, she feels ignored."

"You mean she's spoiled."

"You said it, not me."

"Why can't she understand what we're trying to do here?"

"Well, for one thing, she has a hard time with your work at Sdzeè's."

"I owe her. Without her, I'd be downriver somewhere."

"I know, but Emily doesn't see it that way. To her, Sdzeè is competition—a rival, maneuvering for your affections."

"It's not that way."

"Are you sure?"

"What do you mean?" said Thomas, shifting his chair.

"How do you really feel about Sdzeè?"

"She's...a friend."

Stella smiled at him. He was one of the most upright, ethical men she had ever met, but perhaps he was being a little dishonest about his feelings. "Maybe the way you feel about Sdzeè has changed how you see Emily."

"Like I said, she's just a friend," said Thomas, shifting again.

"I don't know what to tell you, but I'm sure you will make the right decision. Just be honest with yourself and your feelings."

"I'm afraid of how things would change if I break it off, especially my relationship with John—and you."

"Don't worry about that, dear. I will always be on your side, and to be honest, John knows his daughter perfectly well. He's expressed his concerns about her to me."

"The other thing that really bothers me is Declan, do you think he is really your—"

The door opened and Emily half stumbled in, laughing loudly, followed by Declan. At the sight of Thomas and Stella's sudden silence, her look turned sober. Thomas looked away for an instant, hiding the frown on his face.

"Here's your water," said Declan, slamming the bucket down on the table and sloshing a bit over the rim.

Stella cocked her head and gave him a look. "Thanks."

"Having a private conversation, are we?" said Declan.

Thomas resisted the flame of anger growing inside his gut. How he wanted to whirl around and knock that arrogant grin off Declan's face. But he didn't. He got up from the table and faced the pair. "Just letting my food digest. I've got some things to take care of before I call it a day."

Emily said nothing as Thomas brushed past her and left the cabin. "Hmph," she said when he was gone. She sat down in a chair. "Stella, I want tea."

† † †

The morning sun warmed Thomas as he drove the last wedge tight, locking the riffles in place. After days of preparation, they were finally ready to start sluicing the thawed gravels. The plan was to get set up and start sluicing, then get things running on Sdzeè's claim. The biggest decision was how to divide the labor. With two people on each claim, it would be slow going, but that was the only real alternative. Thomas and John had thus far dissuaded Stella from working underground but agreed she'd more than likely pick up a shovel now and then once they started washing gravel. Emily, on the other hand, would no doubt *not* get her hands dirty with any of it.

It was a real quandary for Thomas—deciding where he should work and what to do with Declan. If he worked on Sdzeè's claim, Emily would have cause to be even more difficult. On the other hand, having a respite from the tension would be nice. For a moment he thought car-

ing how she felt wasn't worth it—but he pushed the no-
tion aside. Sdzeè would work her claim, so it was up to
either him or John to go help her. Declan couldn't be
trusted to work without oversight, that was sure.

"We ready to move some gravel?" said John.

Thomas nodded. "I think it would be a good idea
to run some today, just to see if we need to make any
adjustments, then tomorrow go and set up at Sdzeè's."

"Sounds reasonable," said John. "Where are we going to put our illustrious protege?" said John, nodding toward Declan who was leaning against a shovel, cigarette
hanging from his mouth.

"I've given it a lot of thought, and I think it's best you
help Sdzeè with the sluicing. I'll see if I can motivate
Declan to load a wheelbarrow or two here."

"Sounds fine to me, if you're sure you want to take
that on," said John.

"Better than me working at Sdzeè's alone," said Thomas.

John nodded, without stating the obvious.

"Of course Stella can go with you if she wants—no
point in her spending every day here while you're away."

"I'll let her know. I've been neglecting her a bit since
we've been so busy."

"I know, and I feel bad about that."

"It's fine. She understands the effort needed to make
this whole venture a success."

Thomas nodded. "I wish Emily did."

John sighed. "Look, I know it's frustrating, but she
hasn't adapted well. With time I'm sure she'll come
around."

"Are you? I can't even talk to her right now—she's
so jealous, and for nothing."

"That's not the way she sees it."

Thomas sighed, a sinking feeling washing over him. This conversation could go south quickly. He was treading a fine line between father and daughter. When push came to shove, he didn't know for sure where John's loyalties would lie, but he could pretty much guess. *Best leave it alone.* He straightened up. "Well, hopefully, things will smooth out and get better."

"I'm sure they will," said John. He motioned for Declan. "Let's get some gravel moving through this sluice and find some gold!"

Thomas was pleased with their first run of gravel. They spent several hours the day before adjusting the sluice and wing dam to get the flow just right. After about eighteen trips with the wheelbarrow, Thomas estimated they'd run just under two yards of gravel. Not a big run, but enough to proof the setup and make adjustments. Declan kept scratching through the gravel behind the first few riffles, looking for nuggets. John and Thomas repeatedly told him to leave it alone—that he should be shoveling instead of scratching.

Today's task was to set up the sluice boxes at Sdzeè's. Thomas was still a bit worried about their condition since they were idle for two years—maybe more. Sdzeè couldn't remember for sure when they saw gravel last, only that her husband had dismantled them and stored them in the shed before winter—his last winter. Thomas thought about heading over early, but decided against it, waiting to ride along with John and Declan.

Sdzeè was at the tool shed waiting for them when they arrived. She'd already pulled the sluice box segments out and had the riffles laying on the ground next to them, ready for inspection.

Thomas jumped down off the wagon. "Good morning, Sdzeè. Looks like you've been at it early."

"Yes. I wanted to save some time for you."

John and Declan gathered round as Thomas looked over the boxes. They seemed to be in fair shape, although some of the riffle sections needed a little patching up.

"John, why don't you and Declan take the boxes down to the creek and start setting them and build a wing dam if you think it's needed," said Thomas. "I'll get the riffle sections repaired and then we'll be ready to go."

"Sounds like a plan," said John. "Grab the other end of this box and let's get busy," motioning to Declan.

Sdzeè watched them carry the box down the gentle slope to the creek, then turned to Thomas. "How are things?"

"Not bad. I should be able to get these riffle sections fixed up in no time."

"That is not what I am talking about."

Thomas looked at her, then realized the nature of her inquiry. The twinge in his gut confirmed his reluctance to answer.

"I have missed you," said Sdzeè. "I am sorry if I am the cause of much trouble for you."

Thomas shook his head. "It's not you, Sdzeè. It's just the whole situation. Emily is convinced you are her enemy—her rival, and me spending so much time working here hasn't helped."

"I see. I am no one's enemy. I will talk to her."

"I'm not sure that's a good idea. She's really not even speaking to me right now."

"I can fix it for you. I will explain—explain that we are friends—just friends."

Thomas looked at her. She was sincere. Emily had

been in an emotional spiral ever since they left Valdez. The last thing Sdzeè needed was for Emily to assault her with jealous accusations. "No, I will work this out. I don't want you to have to deal with it."

"If you think that is best, but know I will help you in every way I can."

"Thanks, I appreciate that," said Thomas, hoping he could square things without involving her. "Now let's get these riffles fixed and see if we can find some gold."

† † †

By the end of the day, the sluice boxes were assembled and up and running. There was plenty of flow in the creek which allowed them to get by with just a small wing dam made of boulders. After running nearly three yards through the boxes, Thomas called it a day. By then everyone was ready to quit, except Declan, who once again was down pawing through the first riffle.

Declan let out a loud whoop. "Hey look at this," he said, holding up a nugget roughly the size of an apple seed. "I'm rich."

Thomas and John looked at each other—and laughed. "That ain't gonna buy you a mansion, boy, but it's a good sign," said John, holding out his hand.

Declan just looked at him. John motioned with his fingers, palm up. "It's mine," said Declan. "I found it."

"Give it to him," said Thomas. "Now."

With a sneer, Declan reluctantly surrendered the nugget.

"Let me explain to you how this works, as if I should even need to," said Thomas. "We run gravel through the box. We do this for several days—maybe a week. We cleanup and weigh the gold. Then, and only then, we pay you your wage."

Declan grumbled under his breath. "Finders, keepers..."

"It'd be different if you found that laying on the ground somewhere. But the gold on a claim belongs to the claim owners. You're just a hired hand being paid a wage. It will be fair, but none of this gold *belongs* to you."

"Okay, okay, I get it," he said. "Don't have to beat me over the head with it.

I'd like to thought Thomas. *I really would.*

"Looks like we're all set to get into production," said John.

"Almost," said Thomas, turning his thoughts from Declan. "We need to seal up our shaft to insulate it since we're not thawing anymore."

"Ah, right," said John. "Like we did here. Wouldn't want a cave in."

"It should only take a few hours at most to cover it and insulate," said Thomas. "Then we can focus on sluicing and see how it goes. We may have to thaw more, but we'll have to be careful. Most drift miners around here don't work underground during the summer."

"Thanks for the lesson," said Declan. "That was truly enlightening."

Thomas shook his head and headed for the wagon.

† † †

CHAPTER 18

Thomas dumped another wheelbarrow load into the sluice box, washed the bigger rocks clean, and tossed them into the creek. He watched as the current washed the lighter material down the box and out into the creek. Ten days into sluicing, Thomas was contemplating a cleanup. It meant shutting down for the better part of a day in order to shut off the water flow, remove the riffles, and carefully wash all the concentrate into a metal tub. Thomas's plan was to reassemble the sluice box and have Declan continue to feed it while he panned the concentrate to recover and weigh the gold.

Short on cash, they needed to recover some gold in order to buy the materials needed for the house. Thomas thought perhaps having a real house from milled lumber instead of a dirt floor cabin might make Emily happy—or maybe a little happier. He sighed. Trying to run two mining operations and build a house all at once meant long, long days. He thought about hiring someone to help, but at this time of year there wasn't a surplus of labor—everyone looking for work was already employed. Besides, Chicken didn't offer a big labor pool.

Thomas pushed the wheelbarrow back to the stockpile and motioned for Declan, who was sitting on the ground smoking yet another cigarette, to start shoveling. He stood slowly, flicked the cigarette to the ground, and picked up the shovel. *It's a constant battle,* thought Thomas.

He returned to the sluice box and removed the last of the rocks that lingered. It was always a temptation to scratch around in the box—to see what treasure lay behind the first few riffles. He looked to see if Declan was watching, then gently brushed the sand and magnetite aside, revealing a narrow band of bright yellow. *Good, at least we're getting something.* He didn't see any nuggets, but who knows what else the box might hold. Not wanting Declan to get any ideas, Thomas ceased his exploration and returned to help shovel.

"Getting anything?" said Declan.

Thomas realized he wasn't as sneaky as he thought. "I was just tossing out some leftover pebbles, not looking," he said with a white lie.

"Oh, thought you were digging around in there."

"Nope, we don't do that. Don't want to stir things up and risk losing the fine gold."

"Well, I'm looking forward to the cleanup," said Declan. "I want to see if breaking my back is worth it."

Thomas wondered how one could break their back working at a snail's pace. He pitched in, helping to fill the wheelbarrow. "Your turn to dump it," he said to Declan.

Declan pushed the load over the rough ground to the sluice box, spilling handfuls of gravel as he carelessly tipped it from side to side. He successfully dumped it into the box and returned. Thomas wondered how much gold was going to be littered on the ground between the stockpile and the sluice. He'd much rather be working with John or Sdzeè, but that wasn't to be. He looked toward the cabin, wondering what Emily was doing. He thought about inviting her down, to watch at least, but would welcome her help. She was just a slip of a girl, not the kind to be shoveling gravel, tossing rocks, and running wheelbarrows. Still, she could at least show an interest. He wondered how things were going at Sdzeè's. At least Stella went with John—she wasn't shy about getting her hands dirty.

Several times Thomas thought about visiting Sdzeè's claim, but John had assured him things were going well. They were close to a cleanup as well. Thomas hoped to compare the results of both claims—to ensure they weren't wasting their time somewhere. A lot more gravel could be processed if everyone worked on the same claim, but he decided that wasn't likely. He still wasn't sure he was going to accept fifty percent of the take from Sdzeè—it seemed like too much—though he was pretty sure she wouldn't take no for an answer.

"How much longer are we going to run before we cleanup?" said Declan.

"I think we'll do it tomorrow, then probably go help John cleanup as well."

"Good, my back needs a break."

"Don't kid yourself," said Thomas. "Gonna be plenty of work for you in a cleanup."

"Great," said Declan.

The night air was chilled as the full moon lit the landscape. Just after midnight, a lone figure crept slowly along, making sure no noise called out to betray them. They approached the creek, the bubbling of the current welcomed them—it would provide cover.

Taking a small bottle from their pocket in one hand, they began slowly scratching through the first riffle, looking for a telltale glint in the soft moonlight. Slowly the bottle filled, small, smooth chunks of gold adding to its weight. In the second riffle, under a thick carpet of black sand, a nugget the size of a navy bean was revealed. Excited, they worked quicker, finding several more of similar size.

They glanced back at the cabin. All was silent, yet they couldn't be too careful. They fanned the water flowing in the sluice to smooth the material behind the riffles. *Good,* they thought—it looked as it did when they started. Tucking the bottle securely in their pocket, they slowly, quietly, made their way back toward the cabin, smiling all the while.

† † †

Thomas finished the cup of coffee and held it up. Stella refilled it, then returned to making breakfast. It was early—very early, and only the two of them were up. Emily was still sleeping in the bunk, behind a sheet hung to serve as a wall in the one-room cabin. He was glad she was asleep—it was going to be a long day with two cleanups to do and he didn't need any drama. He was amazed at how she could sleep through almost anything. *How could she be so tired when all she did was sit around all day?*

Stella set breakfast before him—eggs, bacon, and potatoes. "We're running low on eggs," she said quietly. "We should probably go to town this week and see if we can resupply."

"How are we doing on other supplies?"

"We should be good for a while."

Thomas ate quickly. He wanted to get out and down to the sluice box before Emily woke up.

"We should think about getting some chickens this

year," said Stella. "A constant supply of fresh eggs would be nice."

"Good idea. Maybe after we get the house built we can build a chicken coop."

Always more work to do, thought Thomas as he stood and put on his coat. "Gotta get to work. I'll wake the others on my way down to the creek."

Thomas slapped the dormitory tent as he passed by, hearing a grunt from John or Declan—he couldn't be sure which. Making his way down to the sluice box, he closed the gate, shutting off the water flow. He dug a hole at the end of the box, deep enough to submerge the metal tub. The current was strong enough around the box that several large rocks from the stream bed were needed to weigh it down. Once the riffles were removed, the tub had to catch all the concentrate or they would lose days of work—and gold.

He added one more rock to the tub to be sure, then started to remove the riffle sections, knocking the wedges loose that held them in place. He carefully tipped each riffle on its side in the sluice box, then used a gold pan to thoroughly rinse the sand and material from them. With all the riffles removed, he was ready to wash all the material from the box into the tub. There were a couple of ways to do it. Either open the gate just enough to flush the box, or do it by hand with a shovel and rinsing with a gold pan. Regardless, he would wait for help. It was important to have somebody make sure everything went in the tub and it stayed put.

Thomas thought about returning to the cabin to roust out the late risers but decided against it. Instead, he gathered up the tools, gold pans, and extra tub, then rolled a cigarette. He turned over the tub and sat down, taking in the last of the sunrise. There was a lot of work to do today, but to be honest, he was at it way earlier than normal. He couldn't fault the others for keeping on the usual schedule. The anticipation of the first cleanup kept him tossing and turning most of the night. They needed to start generating some income, and he felt the pressure.

John arrived, fresh from breakfast. "Ready to get to work?"

"I've already been at it," said Thomas.

"I see that. Declan should be down shortly."

"We can get started without him."

"What's the plan?"

"Well, I hope to get both cleanups done and get back to sluicing by the end of the day. We'll get the concentrate in the tub, then you and I can work on panning it down later. We can reassemble the sluice box and set Declan to sluicing on his own while we head over to Sdzeè's to cleanup."

"Sounds good, but it's going to be a long day."

"We probably won't get down to the final panning today, but if all goes well we'll get both sites back in production, then I can focus the final recovery and weigh up," said Thomas.

"You going to let Declan work alone?"

"I think he can handle it for a day. It shouldn't take more than a day to get everything cleaned up and weighed. It will be interesting to see how much progress he makes unsupervised."

"True. I wouldn't get your hopes up too high."

Thomas laughed. "I know what you mean."

Declan sauntered up, cigarette hanging from his mouth. "Done yet?" he said.

"Funny," said Thomas. "Let's get to it."

John took up the position at the end of the sluice

to ensure the material all made it into the tub. Thomas raised the sliding gate at the head of the sluice to get a little water flow going, then propped it open with a rock. The lighter material began to flow toward the tub. Thomas and Declan used square-ended shovels to scrape the heavier material from the box. The shovels didn't get it all and the remainder had to be washed down by sloshing water on it with a gold pan. Several flakes of gold stuck in the joints between the bottom and sides of the sluice box. Declan was hot to pick those out by hand, which Thomas allowed him to do, as long as he handed them over. Thomas gave the box a final inspection and decided it was clean enough.

The tub was now heavy with concentrate and water. It took two of them to drag it out of the creek. Thomas used a gold pan to bail water out of the tub so it was more manageable, leaving just enough water to cover about fifty pounds of concentrate. They tossed out the big rocks used to weigh it down, then he and John carried it away from the creek and set it near the stockpile.

"You think it will be okay there?" said John.

Thomas nodded. "Let's cover it."

They covered the tub with a canvas tarp and weighted the edges with rocks. "That should be good," said Thomas. "Tomorrow we'll start panning it down. Let's get the sluice setup."

It didn't take long to get the sluice back in operation. Declan wasn't thrilled with working alone, and after a bit of haggling, was successful in convincing Thomas and John to let him go along to Sdzeè's to help with the cleanup. They arrived with the wagon a little after noon. As they approached, they saw Sdzeè down at the sluice box, shoveling gravel.

Thomas stopped the wagon halfway between the cabin

and the sluice box. "Trying to get in that last little bit of gold before cleanup?" he yelled as he hopped off the wagon.

Sdzeè laughed. "There was nothing better to do while waiting for you to arrive."

"Well, let's get busy and see what you've got," said Thomas.

"You mean what we have got," said Sdzeè, correcting him.

"Right," said Thomas as he collected the shovels and tubs from the wagon. "You guys know the drill—let's get at it," he said motioning to John and Declan. *I wonder how John feels when I give him orders?* thought Thomas. *Maybe I should tone it down a bit.*

The cleanup went quicker than at Angel Creek, partially because Declan knew what was expected and stepped up. Thomas found several pieces of coarse gold languishing in the box as they flushed the gravel and black sand into the tub. He handed each to Sdzeè and told her to hang on to them. With the concentrate in the tub and the box reassembled, Thomas declared it was time for a break, with no arguments from the others.

"I am going to the cabin to get a jar for these little nuggets," said Sdzeè.

"Good idea," said Thomas.

Sdzeè headed off to the cabin, while Thomas and John sat on the bench near the shaft, facing the creek. Declan walked a way off and hopped up on the wagon seat. As Sdzeè returned with the jar, she stopped and observed Declan. He was smoking a cigarette, and playing with something. She walked softly forward and saw what it was. He had a small bottle which he was tipping slowly back and forth. As he did, the afternoon sun glinted off the contents. Cautiously nearing the wagon, she could see the bottle was about half full—of gold—nearly two ounces she guessed.

Declan heard her and turned with a start, quickly shoving the bottle into his pocket. He looked toward the shaft—John and Thomas were still relaxing, watching the creek and talking.

"What do you have?" said Sdzeè.

"Nothing. Just a cigarette."

"No, I mean the bottle. What is in it?"

"I don't know what you're talking about—mind your own business."

Sdzeè moved past the wagon without saying a word.

Declan jumped down behind her. "I mean it. Mind your own business. You don't know anything."

Sdzeè nodded. "You are right. I made a mistake."

Declan grinned—message delivered and received. *And yet...*

† † †

With two tubs of concentrate to pan, they decided to take it all over to Angel Creek—there Thomas and John could work on it and weigh it up. Otherwise, it meant Thomas spending time at Sdzeè's, something that would only cause more problems. Sdzeè agreed but wanted to help and be present for the weighing. Thomas wondered if it was better for her to be at their camp with Emily around or for him to spend time at Sdzeè's. *She'll just have to get over it*, he thought. With Sdzeè's help, the panning would go faster.

It was too late in the day to begin work on the concentrate. They agreed to start in the morning.

"What time should I come tomorrow?" said Sdzeè.

"I expect eight would be plenty early, but really, whenever you want to is fine," said Thomas. By then breakfast should be over and Sdzeè wouldn't have to face Emily, assuming she kept up her normal routine and stayed in the cabin all day.

"Good, I can sleep in," said Declan.

"No, you'll be up shoveling gravel."

Declan frowned. "Why?"

"We don't need everyone working on the concentrate. I want you to get back to sluicing."

"Alone?"

"We'll see. John might help once we make some progress on the concentrate."

Declan grunted and began rolling another cigarette.

"Let's get the concentrate loaded and head back," said Thomas. "Sdzeè, we'll see you in the morning."

She watched as they loaded the wagon, then started off. She waved, then called out, "See you in the morning."

† † †

Breakfast was over when Sdzeè arrived. Thomas and John were down near the creek, setting things up to start panning. Declan was nowhere in sight, nor was Emily. Sdzeè was glad for that. She wasn't afraid to face her but didn't want a confrontation for Thomas's sake.

She made her way to the creek, curious about what the others were doing. "What is the process you want to do?"

"Oh, hello," said Thomas. "Glad you could make it."

John nodded in her direction. "Ready to get to work?"

"Yes, how do you usually do it?"

"Pretty simple," said Thomas. "We just take a pan full from the tub and pan it down until most of the sand and little rocks are gone—mainly down to the black sand. We pick out any sizable nuggets and put them in a jar. The rest we put aside."

"Do you use a magnet? That is what we used to do," said Sdzeè, meaning her and William.

"Yes, after we get all the panning done, we'll then separate the black sand with a magnet. Then we dry the rest on the stove, pick out the big stuff, and separate the fine stuff later by hand."

"That sounds similar," she said.

"It works pretty well," said John. "Except when you have a lot of really fine stuff. That gets to be a painstaking process separating it from the little bits of sand."

"Have you considered using mercury in the sluice box?" said Sdzeè.

"Mercury?" said John.

"You add it to the box and it clings to all the gold. Then you burn it off."

Thomas smiled. "I'm impressed. I didn't know you were a mining engineer."

"It is common knowledge," said Sdzeè.

"I've heard of it," said Thomas. "But don't know the details."

"You need a thing called a retort. You heat the mercury and it is driven off. Then you are left with gold. The mercury is distilled in the retort so you can use it again."

"That might be worth looking into," said John.

"There is maybe one problem. All your gold is covered in mercury. If you want to keep nuggets, you have to clean it from them. If you put them in the retort, it becomes a gold sponge."

"Well, we don't want our nuggets covered in mercury. The whole thing sounds messy. It might be worth it if we end up with a lot of fine gold," said Thomas.

"It was only a suggestion," said Sdzeè.

"Oh, don't worry," said Thomas. "It's good to know the alternatives."

Sdzeè nodded. "I have brought gold pans. I am ready."

Thomas scooped up a load of concentrate, walked to the edge of the creek and started panning. "Sdzeè, you can work on the tub from your claim, then we'll help you after we're done," said Thomas.

Sdzeè loaded her pan, then took an empty one and walked to the creek. She set the empty pan on the bank, then dipped the other in the water. She slowly worked the contents of the pan, swirling and dipping it so the lighter material fell into the empty pan.

"What are you doing?" said John.

"Panning."

"I know, but why the other pan."

"William said to always do it this way. Then I will pan again to make sure I have not lost any gold. It is a safety pan. That is what he called it."

John and Thomas looked at each other. *I wonder how much gold we've panned into the creek*, thought Thomas.

"Well that looks like a good idea," said John, grabbing a couple of pans and handing one to Thomas. "Let's do that."

"Right, good idea," said Thomas.

Sdzeè smiled broadly but didn't say anything. *Cheechakos,* she thought.

It took a couple of hours for them to pan the concentrate down. Sdzeè found many nice nuggets—her mason jar was at least three fingers full. Thomas and John, on the other hand, found very few "pickers." The largest was flat, barely the size of a kernel of corn. By the time they were finished, the bottom of the jar was barely covered.

"Disappointing," said Thomas, holding up the jar.

John nodded. "Maybe we'll make it up with the finer stuff."

"I could have sworn there was more coarse stuff in the box," said Thomas.

† † †

Declan finally arrived at the stockpile and began filling a wheelbarrow—slowly. With it half-full, he wheeled it to the sluice box and dumped it in all at once, causing the water to back up and some material to be washed out.

"Declan! How many times have I told you? Feed it slowly," said Thomas.

"Yeah, yeah, I forgot."

"Well do it right. With as little gold as we're getting, we can't afford to lose anything."

"Oh? The cleanup was bad?" said Declan.

"Certainly wasn't what we were expecting," said John.

"That's too bad. Lot's of gravel in that stockpile. Maybe it will get better," said Declan.

"Hope so," said Thomas. "Or we're going to be in trouble."

Declan pushed the wheelbarrow back to the pile and started shoveling, a little quicker this time.

Thomas kept an eye on him as he ran a large magnet over the panned material. The black sands leaped on to it. He scraped it off into another mason jar, careful to make sure no fine gold went with it. After a number of passes, most of the black sand was removed.

"Why are you saving it?" said John.

"Just in case. I want to make sure we aren't losing fine gold with it. I'll look it over later. Here, take our concentrate up to the cabin and see if you can convince Stella to let you put it on the stove to dry it."

John laughed. "Might be a chore, but I'm sure I can convince her," he said with a wink.

John headed to the cabin and Thomas turned his attention to the concentrate from Sdzeè's claim. He ran the magnet over it several times, removing the majority of the black sand. "All we have to do now is dry the rest, get rid of any remaining sand, and weigh it."

Sdzeè nodded.

"You want to come up while we cook this off?"

Sdzeè shook her head. "No, I will stay here."

"It will be fine. You'll have to face Emily eventually."

"I am not afraid to face her—remember I wanted to talk to her and solve the problem. You said no."

"Then why won't you come up?"

"I still have work to do. I want to pan the gravel from my safety pan again. I will come up after—if you are still there."

"Okay, but don't leave without coming up. You need to be there when we weigh the gold."

"I will not leave."

Thomas took the mason jar of nuggets and the panned concentrate of Sdzeè's and headed to the cabin, leaving Sdzeè alone with Declan. She sat several yards away, panning, but watching him as he worked. Each time he started to look at her, she looked down into the pan, avoiding his gaze. By the time Declan dumped several more wheelbarrow loads she was done panning but continued to attentively swirl the pan.

Declan couldn't resist. He pretended to be clearing

rocks from the sluice and fanning the material so it would wash away. Looking back, he saw she was still focused on her stupid pan. He scraped his finger through the first several riffles, finding three nice nuggets—one nearly as large as a nickel. Declan quickly grabbed it, pulled the bottle from his vest, and deposited it.

Sdzeè looked down as he turned her way. He paused, then stared at her.

"Why are you stealing from Thomas and John?" she said.

Declan stepped back, a denial on his lips, but not uttered. He shook his head. "I don't know what you're talking about."

"I saw your bottle yesterday. I saw you take that nugget just now."

"You think you know what you saw, but you better keep your mouth shut—or everyone will be sorry. Making false accusations will bring you a lot of trouble," said Declan, pulling back his coat to reveal the Colt sidearm.

Sdzeè stood and picked up her gold pans. She looked up at the cabin, then back at Declan. He was threatening. Thomas needed to know, but she couldn't be sure what Declan would do in the moment. She decided to wait.

"I will not say anything. It is none of my business," she said, her expression firm.

"You better be telling the truth," said Declan.

"I have seen enough trouble in my time. Gold is not worth it. I will go now."

Declan nodded and waited as she gathered her things, and left, not stopping at the cabin. He smiled, rolled a cigarette, and took out the bottle, tipping it back and forth as he stared at his fortune.

✝ ✝ ✝

Thomas looked around. "Where's Sdzeè?" he said as he returned to the sluice box.

Declan shrugged. "She said she forgot something important and left."

"Without saying goodbye? We're ready to weigh gold."

"I think she wanted to avoid Emily. Pretty sure she's scared of her," said Declan, the lie revealing his ignorance.

"Guess we'll weigh it up and stop by her place tomorrow. We're taking a day off tomorrow and going into town if you want to go. We should have enough gold to pick up some supplies and maybe some lumber for the house."

"A day off—sounds good." Declan rubbed his chin for a moment. "I think I'd like to try hunting again if that's okay."

"John's already not happy with you burning through ammo."

"I'll pay for it out of my cut."

"Okay. This time see if you can't bring back some fresh meat."

"Can I use the horse? I want to cover some more ground."

Thomas wasn't thrilled with the idea but decided maybe Declan had earned a little privilege. "Yes, you can take the old nag. We need the other for the wagon."

"Fine by me," said Declan. "I want to get an early start."

☦ ☦ ☦

CHAPTER 19

It was still dark when Declan rode away. He managed to sneak out without waking the others in the dorm tent. He pushed the nag along the trail, determined to reach his destination before sunrise. John's Model 1873 was in the scabbard, loaded and ready. It was taking longer than he thought—he pushed the horse harder.

The cabin came into view, smoke rising slowly from the chimney. Declan slowed the horse, hopped down, and tied her off to a nearby tree. He pulled the carbine from the scabbard and crept slowly toward the cabin. He stopped and looked at the dog lot. All the sled dogs were holed up in their little houses, still asleep. He moved forward ever quieter. There as a dim light glowing through the window. He hesitated, uncertain if he should knock. He took one last look around, then quietly tapped the barrel of the carbine three times on the door, and waited.

Sdzeè opened the door, saw Declan, and started to speak. Declan rushed her, flinging the door wide open and knocking her to the ground. Suddenly it was upon him—he had forgotten about her dog. Shoh grabbed his arm as he fought to bring the rifle about. The teeth pierced his coat and dug into his flesh. Declan screamed, lifted the rifle over his head and jabbed the butt hard into the dog's skull. Shoh let loose, turned, then lunged at Declan. He fired once, dropping Shoh in his tracks.

Sdzeè was back on her feet and at the sound of the shot she screamed, then reached for her .45-70—but it was too late. The butt of the Model 1873 came down hard on her head and she was out.

Declan checked the dog—it was dead, blood pooled around its head. He quickly fetched a rope from the horse, then rolled Sdzeè over and pulled her hands behind her back. He secured her hands and feet, hog-tying her. He tore a strip of cloth from her shirt and tied it securely around her mouth. He thought of killing her, getting her out of the way. *No, perhaps later. She could turn out to be useful.* For now, she had to disappear.

Declan dragged the dog's body out of the cabin, loaded it on the horse, and rode into the woods.

Sdzeè groaned, her vision blurry, but slowly returning. She tried to sit up but found it impossible. All she could do was roll from side to side. She managed a muffled scream but realized no one would likely hear her. Her head ached, and as she struggled to scoot toward the door, everything went dark.

† † †

Thomas finished hitching the wagon for the trip to town. He was a bit surprised that Declan was gone before everyone else awoke. Seemed to be too ambitious given what Thomas knew of his character. Maybe he was just excited for the hunt—or maybe just glad to miss another day of shoveling and pushing a wheelbarrow.

So far, at least through breakfast, Emily had been agreeable—not overly talkative, but agreeable. Thomas hoped this was a sign that the day would go well. It would be good for everyone to get away from the claim, even if it was a trip to town for supplies. *Maybe we'll have lunch there,* thought Thomas.

Thomas helped Stella up into the wagon. Emily stood for a second, then climbed up. Thomas jumped up and took the reigns, John sitting beside him.

"Everybody ready?"

"Yes," said Stella. "Looking forward to it."

"Well, Chicken isn't the big city, but it's a bit more civilized than our humble abode," said John.

"That's for sure," said Emily. "I haven't seen real civilization since we left Seattle."

"Oh, come on. Valdez wasn't that bad," said John.

"Hmph," said Emily.

"I very much like Valdez," said Stella.

"Oh, I guess it's not that bad," said Emily. "Especially compared to here."

Thomas shook his head, disappointed in her attitude. Perhaps it was time for a talk with John about her—about their engagement. He wasn't sure what he wanted, but it certainly wasn't a life of constant strife—a life that he was living now.

"What all do you want to do in town?" said Stella, hoping to change the topic and lighten the mood.

"I want to go to the sawmill and see if we can place an order for at least some of the building materials we need to get started on the house," said Thomas. "If we have enough gold for the purchase."

Thomas and John completed the final cleanup of the gold the day before. Weighing it, they found Sdzeè's claim did quite well, producing nearly ten ounces of gold, not including the coarse nuggets—not bad for a short run of sluicing. Their claim, on the other hand, produced less than half that, with no nuggets of any size. Thomas couldn't understand why it was such a poor cleanup. Maybe they hadn't got to the richer gravels yet—at least he hoped that was the case.

"Yes, it was a little disappointing," said John. "But it will get better—we've seen some good pans from the workings."

"I hope you're right. I think I need to do more sampling as we thaw next time. That way we won't be running gravel with nothing in it," said Thomas.

"The whole thing seems like a giant waste of time," said Emily, straightening the wrinkles from her dress.

John shot her a glance. "That's the nature of mining and most every endeavor—it takes work and perseverance to succeed."

"Perhaps, but it takes wisdom to know when to quit and cut your losses. I think it's time we return to Seattle," said Emily.

Thomas scoffed at the idea. He wasn't quitting. If she wanted to leave, so be it. Too much time and effort were invested in the claim. He looked at Stella, her face grim—he couldn't read her. He knew John was still onboard, at least he thought he was, yet he was caught in the middle, between his new wife and his indignant daughter.

"It's a little premature to think that way, Emily," said John. "We need to let this play out, at least for the summer."

Emily sighed, twice. It was clear the thought of being stuck for another four months or more did not appeal. Thomas couldn't wait for the wagon ride to be over. He needed to do something about the situation, and it seemed talking to her directly was the only way to straighten it out—if she would be willing and listen. *Not now though.*

They reached the town, and split up. Stella dragged Emily along with her to gather supplies while John and

Thomas went to the sawmill. Thomas hoped the sawmill would accept payment at pickup rather than in advance. It was likely going to cost more than they could afford at the moment. After a brief negotiation, they came to an agreement on a price for materials.

"Gonna be a week at least before I can get at it," said the sawmill owner.

"That's fine," said Thomas, glad they had another week to come up with the payment. He still had the cut from Sdzeè's gold coming. It was up to her to divide it, he wasn't about to presume how much to take.

Arriving back at the general store, they found Stella and Emily waiting for them on the porch. "How did it go?" said John.

"We got a few things we needed, and some fresh eggs. You need to go in and pay," said Stella.

John loaded the wagon and helped the women up while Thomas went in to pay for the supplies. He returned and boarded the wagon, taking up the reins. "Now off to Sdzeè's to deliver her gold," he said, looking back at Emily and Stella. He expected a comment from Emily, but there was silence.

Thomas still thought it strange Sdzeè just left without saying anything the day before—it was so unlike her. Whatever she had to take care of must have been very important. *She'll be happy with the cleanup,* he thought as he drove the wagon onward.

John and Stella chatted along the way—Emily remained silent, staring off across the hills as the wagon bumped along. Thomas figured she was sick of wagon rides, especially after the, in her words, "agonizing" trip from Valdez to the claim.

They arrived at Sdzeè's cabin in the early afternoon. Thomas reined in the horse, jumped down, and tied her off to the post next to the cabin. "Everybody coming in?" he said.

John and Stella nodded—Emily said nothing, just sat in the wagon with her arms crossed.

"We won't be long," said Thomas as he knocked on the door. There was no answer. Thomas thought the silence odd—normally the sled dogs greeted anyone that arrived. He knocked again, waited, then opened the door.

The cabin was empty. "Maybe she's down at the creek," said John. "I'll go look."

"I'll go with you," said Stella.

Thomas nodded and looked about the cabin. Nothing seemed out of place. *She had to know we were coming, why would she leave?*

John and Stella returned from the creek. "No sign of her, and it doesn't look like she's been working down there today. All the tools are still in the shed," said John.

"Odd," said Thomas as he left the cabin and walked around back to the dog lot. All her sled dogs were gone, which was very strange since there wasn't enough snow to run a sled on.

"Do you think she just up and left?" said Stella.

"Doesn't make sense," said Thomas as he went back in the cabin to look around again. "Does that look like blood to you?" he said, pointing to a patch on the dirt floor of the cabin.

John and Stella looked at the dried stain. "Hard to tell. Something's been spilled there but dried and mixed with dirt I can't be sure," said John.

Thomas was starting to get worried, then he noticed Sdzeè's .45-70 was missing from the pegs above the door. "Gun's missing," he said. "If it's gone, she's off somewhere."

"Maybe she headed over to our place," said Stella.

"Maybe—but that doesn't explain why the sled dogs are gone. And where is Shoh?"

"Let's head back and see if she's at our place—or maybe we'll meet her on the way," said John.

Thomas nodded as he untied the horse, then jumped up on the wagon seat.

"I'm sure everything is okay," said Stella.

"I hope you're right," said Thomas. "I really do."

† † †

She rubbed her head, vision blurry, aching feeling, restrained. Slowly she emerged from her fog. At first, what she saw didn't make sense. She felt as though she were below ground. Gradually things came into view. A rusty stove, a bunk, a crude table, sagging roof, and a door that didn't close quite right. She was in a cabin, on the floor, in the dirt, her hands tied behind her back and securely fastened to a post supporting the bunk.

It all came back to her now. The attack by Declan, the shot—*Shoh, oh Shoh!* She cried at the thought of losing the dog, one of the last links to her husband—a dog they picked out and raised together.

She was long wary of Declan—if only she had told Thomas rather than waiting. She struggled against the ropes with no success. *Where am I?* She started to fade again.

The sound outside jolted her back awake. Someone or something was approaching. She peered through the dimness of the musty cabin, hoping to get a glimpse through the rickety door. At the sound of footsteps, she pressed her back hard against the post, digging her heels into the dirt as she pushed.

The door swung slowly open, and the silhouetted figure stepped inside. Her eyes focused—it was Declan. She stared at him. He leaned the .45-70 up against the doorpost. Sdzeè recognized it. She wanted to scream at him—no, she wanted to kill him, but that was not to be—not now anyway. Unsure of his intentions, she waited.

"Hello squaw," he said. "Like your new home?"

She bristled at the term, an offense to her and her people. Again the urge to lash out was almost impossible to ignore, but she resisted. "Why have you done this?" she said, her voice quivering.

"You've become trouble. I know you'll tell Thomas and John about my little high grading operation. I can't have that."

"All this for a little gold. This is too much for so little."

"This is just the beginning, missy. There's more going on here than you know, but unfortunately, you'll not be around to see it."

"More?"

Declan ignored her. "I've got something to cheer the place up for you. I found it lying in the weeds next to the door. I'll get it."

He returned a few seconds later, holding a part of a log about eighteen inches long. It had been split lengthwise, flat on one side. It had two loops of wire on each end from which it could be hung. Declan placed it on the narrow shelf below the window so Sdzeè could see it.

Her eyes strained to read it, then it became clear. Burned into the flat surface of the log was a single word:

HEARTBREAK

"What does it mean?" said Sdzeè.

"Damnation, you are dense, woman. It's from the old trapper that lived here. Apparently this place and what happened here was a heartbreak to him. Looks like he wanted to revel in it. Now it will become the same to you."

"Why do you say that?"

"Because, this is where you die...when the time comes."

"You can let me go. I will not say anything to Thomas."

Declan laughed. "I don't trust you or your kind. Liars all of you."

Sdzeè sneered at him and struggled hard against the ropes.

"Ah, now the true you comes out," he said.

"As have you," she said. "Now what I believed is shown to be true. You are *ts'olniüüdn*."

"English, you ignorant—"

She screamed at him, "The devil, you are evil! You stole my gun—you killed my dog—my Shoh!"

"That's not the half of it. I did the same to your dog team. They're probably halfway down the river by now."

"Tsaan!" she screamed at him, then broke down into tears.

"Don't worry, we're not done yet. Emily may live to see another year, the others, a week perhaps."

"You intend to murder everyone over a little gold?"

"I told you, this is bigger than you think," he said as he picked up the .45-70 and turned toward the door. "Enjoy the night, I have to get back to camp, but I'll see you in a day or two—if the bears or wolves don't get you first."

Sdzeè watched as he left, pushing the rickety door closed as best he could. The sound of the horse faded and she looked again at the trapper's crude sign. Heartbreak—she wondered what led the trapper to create such a thing. Was it because he failed at scratching out a living here? Or was it the loss of a wife, or...?

Heartbreak? We shall see.

† † †

Thomas grew more concerned when they arrived at camp with no sign of Sdzeè. He couldn't understand where she could have gone, especially since she knew they were coming to visit. What made it more disconcerting was the fact all her dogs were gone. Thomas tied up the wagon and headed down to the sluice box to see if there was any sign she had been there. *Nothing.*

He went back up to help unload supplies when Declan came riding up the trail.

"Any luck?" said John.

"Nope," said Declan. "Didn't see a thing."

"Did you happen to see Sdzeè anywhere along the way?" said Thomas.

Declan dismounted and tied up the nag. "No, sure didn't—why?"

Thomas and John explained how they found her cabin empty and all her dogs gone.

Declan looked down, shuffled his feet, then pulled his tobacco pouch out of a vest pocket. "Yes, that is strange. You said her rifle was gone? Maybe she went hunting."

"Doesn't explain why her dogs are all gone. She might take Shoh with her, but I can't see dragging along all the others," said Thomas.

Declan shrugged. "Beats me. Maybe she had a family emergency or someone came with a message."

"I doubt that. She told me she has no one left," said Thomas.

Declan finished rolling the cigarette and lit it. "I'm sure she'll turn up."

"I hope so," said Thomas.

Dinner that night was a muted affair, at least for Thomas. He wasn't interested in the conversation, he was too concerned about Sdzeè. Emily was going on and on about the lack of dress shops in Chicken—an inane topic for a gold mining town of its size.

Emily continued her critique. "I am so disappointed with the lack of entertainment here. I wish—"

"We have to look for her," said Thomas.

Emily looked at him, annoyed at the interruption. "What?"

"We have to look for Sdzeè. Something is wrong."

"You really think so?" said Stella.

"Yes. It's totally unlike her."

"And you're the one that would know, spending most of your days with her," said Emily.

Thomas ignored the bait. He wasn't interested in another argument. "She's a friend and business partner. We need to make sure she's okay."

"Hmph," said Emily. "I don't see why we should have to waste time—"

"Quiet, Emily," said John, deciding it was enough. "Tomorrow we'll look for Sdzeè."

CHAPTER 20

The search began early, Thomas and John taking the horse and wagon along the trail to Sdzeè's. Declan convinced them to let him search the opposite direction to see if perhaps she was headed along the trail to Eagle. Thomas couldn't think of a reason why she would go that way, but, on the other hand, he couldn't imagine why she was missing in the first place.

They arrived at her claim and still no Sdzeè. A quick look through the cabin revealed no further clues as to where she might have gone. Thomas called for Shoh, hoping to at least find the dog, but he didn't appear. Sdzeè may have taken him with her, or worst case, she was hurt somewhere and the dog was standing by her side. It was conjecture, but his imagination flashed a multitude of scenarios before him, none of which ended well.

He was at a loss where to look next. It was John who came up with an idea. "Let's check some of the other mining camps and see if anyone has seen her."

"Good idea," said Thomas. "Let's start with Frank's camp first. He usually knows what's going on around the district."

† † †

Sdzeè strained against the ropes. They were just tight enough that she couldn't get a hand free—but she had to.

Declan would come back and he made clear his intentions. She needed to get free—to warn the others. Her wrists were raw from trying to work free. Frustrated, she lunged forward hard and heard a crack. She pulled again, and more cracking. The bunk post, made of an old, dried out spruce pole, started to give. It might be a way to get free, but it had the potential to bring the entire bunk above crashing down on her head. *It's worth the risk*, she thought.

Lunging forward, the pole gave and she rolled toward the door as the bunk came crashing down. She was free, but her hands were still behind her back. She scooted back, sat on her hands, then rolled backwards, bringing her hands up and over her feet. Standing, she used the rusting edge of the stove to saw through the ropes. She rubbed her wrists, wincing at the pain.

She crept to the door and opened it slowly, realizing that if Declan were anywhere about, he would have heard her crashing escape. She looked around for anything that might be of use but saw only a small, ragged journal underneath the remnants of the bunk. *It must have been hidden somewhere under it*, she thought as she picked it up, looked at the cover, then shoved it into her pocket. *Later.*

Slowly, she stepped out of the cabin. The surroundings were somewhat familiar, yet, she didn't know where she was for sure—it looked like any number of other valleys in the area. She listened carefully, making sure no one was near. She made her way through the knee-high dead grass to the back of the cabin, hoping to get a view that looked more familiar. There in the withered grass, she saw them—two crude crosses, fashioned from dried black spruce. Scrawled on each was a fading inscription—*Beloved wife—Beloved daughter.* So that was it—she now understood the name of the cabin—the source of the trapper's heartbreak. Sdzeè crouched there for a moment, wondering what happened to the old trapper, then she stood in resolve. *This is not to be—Declan will not win.*

† † †

After stops at three mining camps, there was still no word about Sdzeè. Frank called the boys together and inquired. Though they all knew her, none had seen her in days. The same occurred at the other camps, everyone saying they'd keep an eye out for her. By the time they reached Mosquito Fork, Thomas decided it was pointless to continue any further. The word was out, he wasn't ready to give up, but in a country this big, you could spend years searching.

"What now?" said John.

"I guess we head back home, but we'll stop at her cabin again on the way back just in case," said Thomas.

"Makes sense—it's on the way. Maybe Declan found her or got a word from someone."

"Maybe," said Thomas, not convinced of Declan's commitment to any effort. For all Thomas knew, Declan might have spent his "search" sitting back at the claim chatting with Emily. He'd ask Stella how long he was gone.

They arrived back at Sdzeè's and there was no sign she'd been there. Thomas found nothing different in the cabin. In frustration, he took his hat off and threw it to the ground, adding a few choice words in the process. John remained silent until Thomas picked up his hat, dusted it off, and put it on.

"I know you're frustrated, Thomas. She'll turn up—she's

a survivor. Look how long she's been on her own out here."

"I know, but what worries me is no one has seen her and she didn't let anyone know she was leaving."

John couldn't think of anything to allay his fears. "Let's head home. Maybe we'll get some good news."

† † †

Declan urged the horse off the trail and up the creek. He'd only gone far enough down the trail to Eagle to ensure Thomas and the others couldn't see his detour. It took him a while to pick his way along the creek, then up over the ridge into yet another valley. Finally, he dropped into the valley where his prey was waiting. With the detour, he was quite a way downstream from the cabin, instead of coming from above as before. He laughed out loud at the thought of it all—*Heartbreak, how appropriate.*

He made his way up along the creek, wary of being seen. With no mining operation in the valley, he felt pretty confident. The cabin came into view as he approached it from downhill. Something was wrong—the door was open. He kicked the horse in the ribs, closed the remaining distance, and dismounted without tying her up. He grabbed the carbine from the scabbard, worked the lever, and—with the rifle up—entered.

The bunk lay collapsed on the floor, the post broken. The shredded ropes that once held her lay on the floor beside the stove. He burst out the cabin and looked around frantically. *Maybe she hasn't gotten far,* he thought but saw no trace of her. *Where would she go?* There were clearly two possibilities—she either went home or to spill her guts to Thomas. One was a complete disaster—the other he might be able to deal with. *I need to get a handle on this or he is going to kill me,* thought Declan. Yes, after everything, there was no room for error—*he* was going to be furious if it got out of hand.

† † †

With Mount Fairplay as a reference, Sdzeè figured out she was east of her place. She made her way slowly west, careful to stay out of the open as much as possible. Reaching the divide upstream from the trapper's cabin, she could tell she was at the head of Angel Creek. She thought of going to tell Thomas and John what was going on but decided against it—at least for the moment. Walking into their camp with no idea where Declan was could get everyone killed. No, it was best to be careful, to have a plan.

She skirted the ridge above Angel Creek and continued toward her place. Declan could be anywhere, even at her place. Her progress was intentionally slow—she avoided the trail and common routes just in case. The sun was getting low in the sky when she reached her valley, far upstream from the cabin. She slowed even further, sneaking along amidst the stands of black spruce and willow. A hundred yards from the cabin she crouched in the brush and watched. All was quiet, and after twenty minutes, she slowly crept up to the cabin, paused, then entered.

She worked quickly, gathered her warmer coat, some hardtack, a knife, and a blanket. Looking at the pegs above the door that once held her beloved .45-70, she smiled. She opened the chest at the foot of the bed and tossed out the blankets and spare clothes. Prying along the bottom edge, she removed the false bottom revealing

her goal—the Henry repeating rifle and a box of ammunition—a relic of the Civil War era, but still serviceable.

She took the rifle, made sure the action worked cleanly,
and loaded it. It was William's pride and joy from an earlier time. It wasn't the highest-powered rifle around, but
with the .44 caliber round and a close-range target—yes,
if need be, she would make it work. Replacing the false
bottom, she shoved the blankets and clothes back in and
shut it. She shoved the supplies into a pack and peered
out the door. She didn't dare stay too long—it wasn't
safe. Seeing no one, she crept down to the creek, then
sprinted up the valley, weaving in and out of the brush,
hoping against hope that Declan was nowhere near.

As the sun sunk lower, she made it to the head of the
valley, crossed over the ridge and made her way east until
she found the abandoned mining shack. It wasn't much
to look at—she found it while trapping several winters
ago. It stood in a thick stand of spruce and was a rudi-
mentary shelter, with an aging wood stove and only a
spruce pole bunk. She pulled up clumps of moss from
around the cabin and used them to pad the bunk. She
climbed in, pulled the blanket over her, and curled up
with the rifle. Tomorrow she would make a move, but
now she needed rest—and time to think.

† † †

Declan drove the horse hard, racing to find Sdzeè before dark. Riding into camp if she was there didn't appeal
to him—the confrontation had to wait. *Stupid, not tying
her better*, he thought. If he had killed her outright he
wouldn't be in this position, but, despite his disposition,
he wasn't a cold-blooded killer—at least not yet. It might
come to that, if things played out according to plan.

He pushed hard against the fading light, hoping to find Sdzeè at her cabin. Once he skirted the ridge above Angel Creek, he dropped down on the main trail to make better time. If he met Thomas and John, he'd come up with some reason for being there, but hopefully, they had already returned to the claim. The old nag snorted in protest as he pushed her, reaching the cabin as the last rays of light retreated over the rounded hills. He busted into the cabin, rifle ready, but she wasn't there. A twisting pain wrenched at his gut, the reality that she may be at Angel Creek—that everyone knew—tore at him.

He had no choice but to return. Everything depended on it. Declan knew *he* would be furious at yet another of his failures. It could wait no longer—it was time to send the telegram.

† † †

By the time Declan made it back to camp, it was dark. The last mile of the trip was difficult, but the old nag seemed to know the way. He didn't know what to expect, but he spent the entire trip preparing mentally for what he might have to do if Sdzeè was there. *Blast it, if only she hadn't escaped.*

Declan quietly tied up the nag, not bothering to remove the saddle, but then realizing he failed to stash Sdzeè's .45-70 somewhere. It wouldn't do to have that found in his possession. He removed it as someone in the cabin stirred, quickly shoving it far behind the stack of firewood resting against the cabin. He shoved a few logs back to hide it fully, then scooped up an armful. If she was inside, the deal was up—he'd have to suffer the consequences. He stopped, trying to decide if he should go in and finish them all. No, if she was in there, he would do what he did best—lie, discredit, deny, and hope for the best. He reached the door of the cabin just as it opened.

"Where have you been," said Thomas, stepping aside so Declan could enter.

Declan, dropped the firewood next to the stove, relieved that Sdzeè was not among the four in the cabin, then wiped his brow for effect. "Been out searching hard. I've been all over the place, checking some of the valleys, at least the ones where there are trails."

"Did you find anything?"

"Nope, even asked everybody I met. No one has seen her."

Thomas slumped into a chair.

"We didn't have any luck either," said John. "None of the miners have seen her."

"I think we should keep looking," said Declan. "I'd like to go the opposite direction tomorrow and maybe you and Thomas can head toward Eagle. She's got to show up somewhere."

Thomas shook his head, not sure if that was a good idea. He figured she would return either here or at her cabin—he wanted to keep an eye on her place. Then again, given Declan's work ethic, maybe it was a good idea for them to search toward Eagle.

"How far did you go?" said Thomas.

"I made it to about where Atwater Creek comes into the South Fork."

"Hmm," said Thomas. "That's only about four miles. You spent all day until dark and only went that far?"

"Like I said. I searched the valleys too."

"We might as well go that direction tomorrow," said John.

"I'd like to go with you tomorrow," said Stella.

Thomas knew that wasn't a good idea. Not that he didn't want Stella along, but that would leave Emily alone at the cabin and if Sdzeè showed up, there might be fireworks.

"Thanks, Stella, but I really would like to have you here in case she shows up—besides, it's not good to leave Emily here alone, and I'm pretty sure she doesn't want to spend a long day bouncing along in the wagon."

"Thanks for the show of concern," said Emily.

Thomas shook his head. "Okay, we'll all go. We can leave a note for Sdzeè."

Emily protested, "No, I don't want—"

"You'll go," said John. "It'll do you good to get out of this cabin."

"I don't want to help look for her."

"I don't care. You can just sit in the wagon then and stare at your hands," said John. "You're going."

"Hmph," she said, stomping her foot.

Declan laughed. "Glad that's settled."

"I'd rather go with Declan."

"That old nag isn't up to having two people ride her half the day," said Thomas.

Emily sighed, finally relenting.

"How long do we search?" said Stella.

"For another day or so," said Thomas, knowing full well he wouldn't stop until he found her.

CHAPTER 21

Declan burst into the telegraph office in Chicken, nearly tripping over the threshold.

"You okay, mister?" said Wayne, looking up from the telegraph key.

"Yeah—fine. I need to send a telegram immediately."

"Sure, just jot the message down on the pad here."

Declan grabbed the pad and quickly scribbled out the message. Wayne took it and counted up the words. "Okay, that'll be four bits."

Declan grumbled, dug into his pocket and came up with the coins. Wayne took the money, then shoved the message to the bottom of the stack.

"What gives?" said Declan. "Aren't you going to send it?"

"I'll get to it eventually. I've been busy getting incoming messages and I haven't had my third cup of coffee yet. Been pretty slow these last days so I like to pace myself, otherwise, there's nothing for me to do."

Declan frowned. "That needs to go out—now!"

Wayne picked it up and read it:

```
COLE BRADLEY / KECHUMSTUK ALASKA
IT'S TIME. COME NOW. DO NOT DELAY.
DECLAN / CHICKEN ALASKA
```

"Hmm, looks sort of urgent—maybe," said Wayne.

"What's it about?"

"That's none of your blasted business," said Declan. "Are you going to send it or not?"

"Sure mister, don't get your bloomers in a wad."

Declan's fists tightened as he stared at him, knowing he was at his mercy. The message had to be sent—pummeling the telegraph operator wouldn't help. He switched tactics.

"If I throw in a little extra can you move it to the top of the stack?"

Wayne looked at him, looking for a hint. "How little?"

"Here's another two bits," said Declan, slamming them a little too hard onto the counter.

Wayne looked down at them, then back up at Declan. He said nothing, just stared.

"More?"

Wayne nodded.

Declan felt the blood rushing to his temples, the veins beginning to bulge. He slapped another pair of coins on the counter.

"Done," said Wayne, scooping up the money and pulling the message from the pile. He smiled at Declan. "That's our fee for expedited service. Sending now."

Declan stood there, watching. He wasn't about to be cheated and wanted to ensure the message actually went. In less than a minute, Wayne stopped sending.

"That's it?" said Declan.

"Yup, it went. Received in Kechumstuk. No guarantee when this...uh...Bradley fella will get it. Up to him to come fetch it from the office there."

Declan grunted and left the office, slamming the door behind him.

"Grumpy fellow," said Wayne as he leaned back in his chair, arms folded behind his head.

☦ ☦ ☦

Telegram sent, Declan proceeded west on the trail, destined once again for Sdzeè's. It was great fortune that the others fell for his suggestion to search west toward Eagle, thus allowing him to send the telegram and continue his search for Sdzeè in the most likely place—her claim. Unsure of what to do if he couldn't find her, his only hope was that Bradley would come quickly. After all, this was his show—his grand plan. Declan wondered if it was all worth it, but the vision of his bottle filled with nuggets reassured him.

He met only two strangers on the trail and asked both about Sdzeè just to cover his tracks. *You never know who knows who.* The trip from Kechumstuk was a hard day's ride, more likely two depending on the trail. Declan wasn't sure he could hold out for two days. It all depended on Sdzeè. *Where was she?* He thought sure she would run to Thomas and that would be the unraveling of everything. A sudden twinge of optimism came over him. Maybe she was dead, mauled by a bear, attacked by wolves, drowned in a creek. That would be ideal—in fact, making her death look like an accident would clear him—no questions asked. But he first had to find her.

He arrived at her claim, checked the cabin, then rode up the creek, past the new shaft and beyond. *Maybe she's hiding underground.* He returned to the shaft. It was still covered and insulated, just as they left it when the equipment was pulled out and moved to Angel Creek. Declan considered uncovering it and looking but thought better of it. If she was hiding down there, she likely died from lack of air long ago. Besides, uncovering the shaft, climbing down, then replacing everything to look undisturbed seemed like way too much work.

That left only one possibility—she was out there in the wild somewhere. What did she know of the area, he wondered. All the little places one could hide—the abandoned mines, vacant cabins, shacks—she probably knew them all. He mounted up and headed further west, hoping fate would smile upon him.

† † †

After a restless night, Sdzeè packed up her meager gear and headed east toward Angel Creek, keeping off the trails to avoid discovery. She wrestled all night with what to do. She decided the safest thing was to get to someone from Thomas's camp and let them know what Declan planned. Busting into camp with Declan present could result in a bloodbath. She had to make sure he was not around when she marched into their camp.

The other concern, of course, was the amount of time she had before tragedy struck. He mentioned a week, but she couldn't trust anything he said. She continued on her way, ever careful of her surroundings. She didn't know what Thomas and the others were doing, but she was pretty sure Declan was looking for her—as long as he could make an excuse to get away.

Reaching the ridge above Angel Creek, she stopped and sat down on the gentle slope, surrounded by low brush. She could see the cabin and the sluice box, but there was no activity. It was mid-morning—if they were about she would expect to see them working. She worked her way slowly down the slope, pausing frequently to look and listen.

As she reached the creek, she stopped—the wagon and horses were gone. She stood, hoping this meant that everyone—at least Declan—was gone. She crossed the creek, crept up behind the cabin, and listened. No sounds. She raised up and looked through the window. From what little she could discern, it was empty. She worked her way around to the front and slowly opened the door. To her relief, it was empty, but it would have been much better if Thomas or John were there.

Next, she moved to the dormitory tent, once again walking slowly and listening. Hearing nothing, she entered the tent. She stood and relaxed, at least for the moment. Though she felt like an intruder, she looked around, hoping to find something that would give her a clue as to Declan's vague insinuations about a bigger plot. On one of the cots, the messiest, was a canvas bag she recognized as Declan's from when the group first arrived in Chicken.

She opened the bag and began looking through the contents. Tobacco, dirty shirt, matches, other clothes, and, clear at the bottom of the bag, an envelope. She opened the envelope, revealing a couple of newspaper clippings, several dollars, and a single note on a slip of paper. She looked at the clippings, both from a newspaper in Seattle. The first talked about the good mining season in the Fortymile during 1902. To her surprise, the other clipping, a brief snippet among other items, was dated January of this year:

> Rumor from Valdez Alaska has it that Messrs. Thornton and Palmer have uncovered rich gravels on their claim at Angel Creek in the Fortymile. They are said to be opening up the drift mine according to sources in Valdez.

Interesting. She replaced the clippings and read the note:

```
This is it Cullen, my boy. Contact me
when the time is right. This will be
our biggest play. Good luck.
              ~S
```

She studied it for a second, then carefully replaced it in the envelope. The clipping and the note raised more questions than they answered. It was clear that Declan was there for the gold, but who was Cullen? And who had written the note—who as *S*? *Stella?* No, that made no sense. She turned the envelope over and over—both sides were blank. *No clue here.*

She made sure everything was replaced in the bag as she found it—except the envelope. She paused, trying to decide if she should keep it—show it to Thomas. She started to put it back in the bag, then stopped. She would keep it. If she was lucky, Declan wouldn't notice since it was under all his other belongings. It was a risk, but then again, she had little to lose at this point.

She had to find Thomas and John, and avoid Declan at all costs. When the time was right, she would reveal herself, but for now, she had to remain patient, watch, and wait. She left the Angel Creek camp, climbed the long slope to the ridge top, and made her way to a safe place—a place where Declan could not find her.

† † †

Declan was the first to return to camp after his day of searching. After leaving Sdzeè's camp, he'd traveled further west and visited several other mining camps, each affirming they'd not seen Sdzeè. On the way back, he stopped at her camp, just to be sure. Once again he hoped she was dead, a victim of a bear attack or something worse. *I hope she suffered,* he thought as he dismounted, tied up the nag, and retrieved the .45-70 from behind the woodpile. He had to find a better hiding place before the others returned. Keeping it in camp wasn't an option—it would be too easy for someone to stumble across it—explaining it would be impossible.

He hiked up the hill behind the cabin, looking for a spot to temporarily hide the rifle. He came to a thick section of scrub brush and fallen spruce, dragged several of the dead trees together, and placed the rifle underneath. To ensure it was hidden, he broke off some spruce boughs and placed them around the hiding place, trying to make it not too obvious. There was no reason for anyone to come up the hill anyway, so he was confident in the hiding place. Taking one last look, he headed back downhill.

Declan emerged from the little stand of trees directly behind the cabin to find Thomas and John staring at him. He wondered why he didn't hear the wagon when they returned.

"We saw you were back," said Thomas, pointing at the nag. "What were you doing up there?"

Declan laughed at him. "You sure are nosy. Can't a guy do his business without everyone knowing about it."

Thomas ignored the answer and set about taking care of the horse and wagon. Stella and Emily were already in the cabin, and Thomas prepared himself for another not-so-delightful experience at dinner. Declan started for the cabin.

Thomas stepped in front of him. "You rode the horse, now take care of her. Get that saddle and blanket off and brush her down. I did it for you yesterday for her sake. If you can't take care of her you can walk everywhere from now on."

"Boy that missing squaw sure has you on edge," said Declan.

He didn't see it coming. Thomas landed his fist square on Declan's jaw, knocking him backwards against the woodpile. Declan staggered to recover, fists clenched. Before he got his balance, Thomas double-punched him hard in the stomach, knocking the air out of him. He went down and rolled on his side. Thomas stepped forward, foot raised over him.

"Stop it!" yelled Stella. "Stop it right now!" she screamed just as John moved between Thomas and the incapacitated Declan.

At the sound of Stella's command, Thomas backed off, rubbing his fist.

"That's Wesley's son. You can't do that to him," said Stella between sobs.

"He called Sdzeè a—"

"I don't care. I love you Thomas, but you can't go on like this," said Stella.

John helped Declan up. Despite being beaten, he sneered at Thomas. *Your time will come,* he thought, but for now, maybe he could play this to his advantage. He groaned and walked doubled over as Stella took him by the arm and helped him to the cabin.

John looked at Thomas and shook his head. "I think you took that a little too far."

"Maybe." Thomas didn't think so, he thought Declan deserved much more. Stella's sudden concern over him surprised Thomas a bit, but then she was a peacemaker. Now he wasn't sure about anyone's loyalties.

John started to remove the saddle from the nag.

"I'll do it," said Thomas. "I'll take care of both of them. Go on inside."

"I'm happy to help."

"No. Let me. It will give me time to cool down and

think."

John nodded and headed into the cabin. Thomas took a deep breath, rubbed his sore fist once more, then set about caring for the horses. He finished brushing down both and took care of the tack, then sat down on the big log they used for splitting firewood. He rolled a cigarette and sat there, staring out over the valley. *What a mess,* he thought. All of it, Declan, Emily, Sdzeè missing—it was all too much. He finished the cigarette, crushed it out with his boot, and sat there, staring.

The cabin door opened. "Dinner," said Stella. "Come along Thomas."

"Not hungry."

Stella came out and around to where Thomas was sitting. "Look, I'm sorry I screamed at you, but it had to stop."

"I don't like him, and I don't like the way he talks about Sdzeè," said Thomas.

"I know he can be a bit brash, and a bit of a chore to be around, but you have to remember his background—his growing up without parents and now having no family of his own."

"Does that give him an excuse?"

"No, but with time he could change. We just have to be patient. You know it's only because of Wesley that we brought him along—to try and be family to him. I think we owe him that much."

"I know. And he is closer relation to you than I am."

"Thomas, don't. You know I love you like the son I never had."

"I can never repay you for what you did for me when I first arrived in Valdez—after I was shot. But maybe it is better if I go my own way—you have a new life with a husband and Declan."

"Thomas, don't talk like that. That's not where my heart is at all. Come, let's eat. Dinner is ready. We can talk about this more later, but now, let's all just get along."

Thomas looked at her standing there—she reminded him of his mother. He loved her, but the pressure lay heavy upon him. He looked down.

"Come," she said, reaching out with her hand.

Thomas turned away. "I'm not hungry."

CHAPTER 22

Thomas was up early the next day, hoping to avoid a conflict. His altercation with Declan only made the situation in camp worse. He didn't like him but had to tolerate him for Stella's sake. After laying awake a better part of the night, he came to a decision—there must be a heart to heart talk with Emily—to reconcile where their relationship was headed, if anywhere. Furthermore, as much as it galled him, he would apologize to Declan. As for Sdzeè, two days of searching proved fruitless—it was time to get back to work. If nothing else, it would take his mind off things. Still, he hadn't given up on her.

Thomas entered the cabin, finding Stella already drinking a cup of coffee. She was always up early, always working, always helpful and supportive. Emily was awake, sitting on the edge of her bunk. She looked away as Thomas poured a cup of coffee from the pot on the stove and sat down at the table.

"How are you feeling today?" said Stella.

His hands were clasped around the cup, his eyes avoiding hers. "Look, I'm sorry about yesterday. I feel like everything is falling apart around me."

"We are fine, Thomas."

He looked up. "Emily, we need to talk."

Emily stared at him. He waited. "What do we have to talk about, Thomas? About you ignoring me, about your

Indian girlfriend, about your unfaithfulness to me?"

He felt his temper flare. *Was it even possible to have a conversation with her?*

"You need to give Thomas a chance—you two need to work this out," said Stella as she stood and put on her coat. "I'm giving you some privacy—better talk while you can, the others will be wanting breakfast soon."

With Stella gone, silence reigned over the cabin for a solid minute. To Thomas if felt like much longer. Finally, he spoke. "Emily, we need to set some things straight. I haven't been unfaithful to you."

"It seems like it to me. You've spent so much time with her."

"Yes, time with her—with John and Declan there as well. It's not like I'm spending time alone with her."

"You did before we got here. I know that for sure."

"Yes, but she was helping me get ready for your arrival. It was all above board."

"I'm not sure I can trust you."

"Well, you certainly haven't been very pleasant—and I've seen you carrying on with Declan."

"An innocent flirtation," said Emily.

"And you think that's fine? To carry on with him that way?"

"Hmph," said Emily, looking away.

"So where do we go from here?"

She looked up at the ceiling, then crossed her arms. "I don't know."

Thomas hesitated to say it but knew it had to be done. "Do you still want to get married?"

"I...don't know."

"Maybe we should wait," he said.

"Call off the engagement?"

"If you wish," said Thomas.

Emily stared at him, her eyes narrowed. "Why can't you take a stand on anything?"

"You're being unreasonable."

Emily ripped the modest engagement ring from her finger and threw it at him. "How's that for unreasonable?" she said.

"I have my answer," said Thomas as he picked the ring up off the floor. "I hope someday you'll be happy," he said as he reached the door, gave her one last look, and left.

Emily stared at the closed door, put her face in her hands, and started to cry.

† † †

Thomas dumped another wheelbarrow load into the sluice. After the confrontation with Emily, he immediately got to work, hoping it would get his mind off it all. Stella brought him a plate of food, not even bothering to try and get him to come up for breakfast. Now he waited for John to come down, dreading the conversation that was imminent—hoping that Declan tarried.

He just finished washing clay off some of the larger rocks stuck in the sluice when he heard someone approaching. He turned to see John standing there, hands in his pockets. The look on his face was hard for Thomas to read. "Talk to Emily?" he said finally.

"Yes."

"I'm sorry John. I'm sorry for everything. I suppose this is the end of our friendship."

"It's not your fault, Thomas. Emily has been through a lot, losing our home, our fortune, her mother. I'm afraid it's all just too much for her."

Thomas nodded, unsure of what to say.

"Let's face it, she's not the pioneer type. I don't know all that's gone on between you, but I know most of it."

"You do know all of it. I've not been unfaithful to her."

"She wants to leave. Stella is talking to her now, trying to calm her."

"What will you do?"

"Well, Thomas, you know I'm kind of stuck in the middle here."

"I know. If you need to leave I understand. I can try and make enough this summer to buy out your share of the mine—whatever you think is fair."

"Let's not go there just yet."

"What does Stella want to do?"

"She hasn't said and I haven't had a chance to talk to her alone. She's in an awkward position as well—between you and her new family."

Thomas nodded, then pulled the gold band from his pocket, holding it up for John to see. "She threw this at me, you know."

John frowned. "No, she didn't tell me that. Do you think there's any hope for reconciliation?"

"I don't know. To be honest, I think it will take time to see where the relationship goes, if anywhere. For now, I think we should leave it as is," said Thomas.

"I understand. I don't really want to return to Valdez—at least not yet. I think you've got the right idea getting back to work—I could use a diversion as well," said John as he picked up a shovel.

Thomas pushed the wheelbarrow back to the stockpile and they began shoveling. Thomas wondered when

Declan would come down—if he would come down—and how that would play out. He didn't have to wait long, after two wheelbarrow loads, Declan came sauntering down the hill, smoking a cigarette. Thomas dreaded his arrival.

"Ready to get to work?" said John as Declan arrived.

Declan looked at Thomas, grunted, said nothing. He was sporting a lovely bruise on his jaw, the result of Thomas's handiwork. Thomas felt sorry—not for Declan, but that he lost his temper.

Thomas drew a deep breath. "Declan, I'm sorry about yesterday. I hope you can forgive me," he said, trying to sound as sincere as possible.

Declan crossed his arms. He could play this two ways—make peace and pretend to get along or escalate things. He remembered the telegram, the plan, and decided it was best to back down—at least until *he* arrived. Declan relaxed his arms, then smiled. If Thomas only knew what happened to Sdzeè, he'd have more than a bruise.

"Yeah, okay," said Declan. "I should've kept my mouth shut too," he said as he offered his hand.

Thomas hesitated, then shook his hand, engaging in a short battle to see who could crush the others first.

"Good," said John. "Now let's get to work."

The three worked hard through the morning, conversation at a minimum. Thomas was surprised at Declan's energy. He wasn't his normal, sluggish self, and didn't need nudging to keep moving. Though pleased with the amount of material moved through the sluice, Thomas's thoughts kept returning to Sdzeè. On one hand, he felt bad about the encounter with Emily, but on the other, he could now pursue searching for her without guilt—after all, he was already judged guilty. He had nothing to lose, at least when it came to Emily. She was the one who broke it off.

Stella brought lunch down to the sluice. Emily was still holed up in the cabin. Thomas wondered what she could possibly do all day—no wonder her mood was foul—she had nothing to do but sit and stew.

Stella gently took Thomas aside. "You know Thomas, you can't avoid her. We still need to have meals together, at least in the evening."

"I know, but it's not easy."

"I understand. Perhaps she'll soften a bit. I'll talk to her."

"Please do, and see if you can find out what she really wants. It seemed so abrupt—her throwing the ring at me."

"I know."

Stella sat for a spell while they got back to sluicing. She watched the three men in her life as they worked. Thomas and John she knew well—Declan was still a bit of a mystery. *So unlike Wesley, his father*, she thought. His work ethic was weak, his attitude at times sour, and he was often disrespectful in his comments. How she wished she knew the full story of Wesley's relationship with Declan's mother all those years ago. She never suspected he was unfaithful, and each time she looked at Declan, a twinge of sorrow followed—not that it was his fault. He was here because of her, and yet she began to wonder if it was a mistake.

She walked slowly back up to the cabin, then turned and looked back at the three working. *Everything will be alright*, she thought as the entered the cabin.

† † †

With three of them working, they managed to run

twice the usual amount of gravel through the sluice. Several nice size nuggets were found at the head of the box, heavy enough they didn't even travel as far as the first riffle. Thomas and John placed each in a large jar they kept by the sluice. Thomas was ecstatic—they were finally in the pay. Just one day's work and they were far ahead of the last disappointing cleanup.

As the day wore on, tensions between Declan and Thomas eased—in fact, he even let Thomas know each time a nice chunk of gold appeared at the head of the box.

"This claim just might pay for itself," said Thomas.

"Yes, it's looking good today," said John. "Let's just hope it continues."

Thomas picked up the jar of nuggets and held it up in the afternoon sun. A sadness swept over him.

"What's wrong?" said John.

"Just thinking about Sdzeè. I haven't given up on her. I know Emily will be mad—or maybe she doesn't care anymore, but I think tomorrow I'm going to work half a day, then let you and Declan continue while I go to her claim once more. Maybe even into town to ask around again."

"I understand," said John. "I'll go with you."

"No, we need to keep sluicing. We can't afford to shut down completely. If I can't find any sign of her tomorrow, I guess I'll have to let it go."

"Alright," said John. "Maybe she did have something come up that explains her absence."

"I hope so, but why didn't she let us know—didn't even leave a note."

"Maybe it happened suddenly," said Declan, leaning on a shovel.

"That would seem to be the only explanation," said

John.

Declan suppressed a grin. "What becomes of her claim now?"

Thomas's eyes narrowed. "It's a little early to be asking that question."

"Right, I mean, what if she never comes back? It's half yours so I guess you become the owner."

Thomas glared at him. There was no formal documentation of their business agreement, but that was the last thing on his mind. Obviously Declan was thinking otherwise, maybe hoping for a windfall. "I'm not thinking about that—the claim's not important, her well-being is."

A smug look spread across Declan's face. "Right, of course. How inconsiderate of me."

Thomas couldn't tell if that was sarcasm or just more of his brutish sense of humor. Or maybe he cared for no one but himself. Despite a good day of working with him, Thomas's feelings about him were unchanged.

"Let's finish up with a couple more loads and call it day," said Thomas, ending the conversation.

"Sounds good to me," said John. "I'm getting hungry."

† † †

The door of the telegraph office swung open wide, banging loud against the stop. Wayne nearly fell out of his chair, startled awake by the noise. He regained his composure, adjusted his spectacles, and examined the source.

Before him stood a grizzled looking fellow, a graying beard down to his collarbone. His shoulder-length hair stuck out under his ragged leather hat. On his hip was a gun belt, and in the holster, what looked like a Colt Single Action Army revolver. Wayne stepped back from the counter. "Uh...can I help you?"

"Yeah, matter of fact you can. You got any messages for Cole Bradley?"

Wayne shook his head.

"Don't you need to look?"

"No, nothing's come in for you, but I remember sending one for you the other day. I see you made it here pretty quick."

Bradley glared at him, unhappy with the intrusion into his affairs. "Best mind your own business," he said, patting the butt of the .45.

Wayne nodded and took another step back. "Uh...sorry."

"Where can I get a room?"

"There's a boarding house just down the street. Pretty sure they can put you up for the night," said Wayne, his voice quivering.

Bradley rested his hand on the Colt. "One other thing you can help me with..."

Wayne nodded vigorously, "Anything, mister, anything you want."

"I need directions to Angel Creek."

CHAPTER 23

Sdzeè shivered in the dim, early morning air. Her second night in the abandoned mining shack two valleys from Angel Creek had been even more restless than the first. She spent the day before on the ridge above the Angel Creek claim, watching and waiting for an opportunity to sneak in without Declan around. She watched as all day they ran gravel through the sluice, with never an opportunity to safely approach. She wished Thomas or John would leave the claim—go to town or something—so she could intercept, but it was not to be.

She thought about returning to her cabin, but dismissed the idea—it was too much of a risk. Declan was unpredictable and she would not allow him to get the advantage again. She could risk it and just show up at the camp, hoping that Declan wouldn't do anything crazy when she appeared. The last thing she wanted was a massacre. *Maybe I'm being too cautious.* Soon she would have to decide. Based on what Declan said when she was captive, time was running out.

Sdzeè gathered up her pack and the Henry, then started the hour hike to the ridge above Angel Creek for another day of waiting. She was pretty sure Declan had given up looking for her, but still she was cautious, avoiding open areas as much as possible—moving slowly and quietly. The hike warmed her, as did the spring sun as it came up over the hills. After a brief rest stop, she reached the ridge above Thomas's claim, tucked herself into a small stand of willow, and surveyed the valley. She needed a way to approach—to get closer so she could have the upper hand if it came down to a confrontation with Declan.

On the same side of the creek as her, not far from their sluice box, was a granite tor—a monolith of rock standing alone below the last bench of the valley. It wasn't huge, she estimated ten feet across and maybe fifteen feet tall. If she could sneak down to it, it would put her close to the camp and provide cover. Making it into their camp would then be just a short run and wade across the creek. The only issue was, once she was at the tor, she would have to remain until dark. There was no way to retreat without risking being seen.

It was light out, no sign of activity from the camp. *They are probably at breakfast*, she thought—she hoped. It was now or never. She grabbed her pack and dashed down the hill, half crouching and weaving among the short stands of brush, knowing full well that her motion would betray her if anyone looked across the creek. She made it to the rock outcrop and leaned against it, gasping for breath from the sprint. She waited for her breathing to slow, then listened. Nothing. She moved to the right side of the outcrop—a small stand of pucker brush provided a bit of cover through which she could observe the sluice box and the cabin. Still no activity. She moved back behind the outcrop and settled in—waiting.

The sound rang across the early morning quiet of the valley, jarring Sdzeè awake. She stiffened, her hand on the rifle. There it was again—she crawled to the edge of the outcrop and peered through the brush. Voices now, carrying across the sound of the creek—it was Thomas and John. The noise—the crashing of gravel against the metal bottom of the wheelbarrow. She rubbed her eyes. *How long have I been asleep?* The sun wasn't much higher—not long she judged. She got to her knees. This might be her chance if she hurried. She stood, stepped around the outcrop ready to run just as Declan exited the cabin. She dropped like a stone, flat on her belly, trying to blend into the moss and lichen. She was sure he'd seen her. Slowly she turned her head, raising just enough to look. Declan was looking down at the ground as he walked, a cigarette hanging from his mouth. If he saw her there was no sign. She quietly retreated behind the outcrop, inching backwards while on her stomach.

There was a way to solve this—inside a hundred yards with the Henry was doable, if she was careful. One shot and Declan would be out of the picture. She belly-crawled again to the edge of the outcrop, pushing her pack in front of her. Reaching the edge, she shoved the pack ahead of her, still hidden behind the stand of brush. She laid the Henry across the pack, adjusted her position, and aimed. He was a big enough target at 70 yards. She put the post of the front site squarely in the middle of his chest. Her finger wrapped slowly around the trigger, she took a deep breath, began to exhale, then started to shake—uncontrollably. *I can not do this.* Self-defense was one thing, this seemed like cold-blooded murder. Her finger slipped from the trigger and her body went limp. She lay there in the moss, breathing slowly, waiting for the shaking to stop. *There must be another way.*

† † †

The day grew long, with no opportunity for Sdzeè to approach—no opportunity to tell of Declan's treachery. She mentally kicked herself again for delaying, but Declan's ever-present sidearm was her main concern.

She watched as they finished up the day's labor. The sun would set in a little less than an hour, and she needed to decide where to spend the night. The thought of sleeping in the open next to the outcrop didn't appeal much, especially with the chance, though remote, of being discovered. She could wait until they were asleep and try to sneak up to the dorm tent—to try and get Thomas's attention, but that would be risky.

She was hungry—she was tired of waiting. She remained until the three retreated to the cabin, then headed up the hill in the fading light, destined for the abandoned shack. As she reached the top of the ridge, she sat down among the brush to catch her breath. She looked back at the creek, straining to make out the details as the sun dipped below the hills. There at the sluice was a sole figure, indistinguishable in the fading light, bent over and scratching through the concentrate. *Declan, no doubt*, but she couldn't be sure. *One way or the other, this ends tomorrow*, she thought as she stood and pressed on—quicker now.

† † †

Declan stood from the dinner table. "Well, I'm going to take a little walk—get some fresh air."

"It's dark out," said Stella.

"I know, but there's enough moonlight."

"Watch out for bears," said Emily.

Declan patted Colt in its holster and smiled. "I'm ready," he said as he opened the door.

"Which way you going in case we have to come look for you?" said John.

"Just down the trail aways—not far."

Thomas watched as Declan closed the door, then looked

at John. "That's something new. Second night in a row he's gone for a little walk."

John shrugged. Thomas got up from the table and looked out the cabin door. Indeed, Declan was sauntering down the trail that led to Chicken, a cigarette hanging from his mouth. He shut the door and returned to his chair.

"How's he been working out?" said Stella.

"Not bad," said Thomas. "But you have to keep after him most of the time to keep him motivated."

John shook his head in agreement.

"He probably hasn't had much structure in his life given his past," said Stella. "I think this has been good for him."

"Certainly hasn't hurt him any," said John.

"In time I'm sure he'll come around," said Stella.

"Hope so," said Thomas, not really confident Declan would ever be an asset to their operation. He stared down at the steaming cup of coffee Stella poured for him as his mind drifted to thoughts of Sdzeè. Somehow he had to find her—or at least find out what happened to her. He wouldn't mention it in front of Emily, but tomorrow he planned a trip to town and her cabin, hoping for at least a clue, a word, that would lead to finding her.

† † †

Once out of sight of the cabin, Declan quickened his pace down the trail. Without an idea of when Bradley would show, he decided that taking "walks" was the only way to meet up and give him the scoop before proceeding. The plan called for Bradley to arrive an hour or two after dark, he just didn't know which day.

Declan didn't like the long game, preferring to get on

with it and move on. This had been the longest con of his career, but he had to admit, it was well-conceived.

He didn't want to go too far, the night air was chilly, and after all, it was more effort than he wanted to expend, especially after shoveling all day. He reached the bend in the trail just before a long hill that descended to the valley floor. He stopped next to a fallen spruce, sat down, and rolled a cigarette. He would wait—just long enough to appease his conscience—and provide an excuse.

Two cigarettes later, Declan stood and peered down the valley. In the moonlight, he could only see about a quarter-mile of trail before it rounded another bend. He turned and started back toward the cabin, then stopped for one last look. Coming into view was a horse and rider, moving slowly toward him. He felt the tell-tale twinge in his gut. *It had to be him.* No one else would be coming to Angel Creek this time of night. Declan faded back into the brush next to the trail and waited, the Colt at ready.

The rider approached and slowed his pace. Declan watched, still unable to determine their identity. The horse stopped next to the fallen spruce. "You can come out my boy. It's me."

Declan stepped through the brush. "How did you know?"

"The cigarette butts, spent matches, and fresh tracks. Figured no one else would be standing in the bushes this time of night."

Declan laughed. "Never could get away with any-thing, even when I was little—at least when you were around."

Bradley ignored the comment. "Is everything set?"

"Well, there's lots of gold in the box and everyone is at camp."

"How many?"

"Four of them, but there could be a slight little problem," said Declan.

Bradley sneered. "What?"

Declan went on to explain in detail Thomas's partnership with Sdzeè, then revealed how she caught him stealing gold from the sluice. Bradley listened, a frown firmly fixed on his face. The part about the kidnap and escape of Sdzeè wasn't taken well.

"Blast it, boy. How could you let that happen? Where is she?"

"I don't know. Everyone looked for her for several days with no sign of her. I think a bear or something got her. Surely she would have showed up by now."

"You should have found her. This could be a problem."

Declan shook his head. "Nah, I think she's gone, one way or the other. I looked all over for her."

Bradley mounted up. "How far to the cabin?"

"Half mile at the most. We doing this now?"

"Yeah, I'm not going to sleep out in the woods. We need to move ahead, and quickly."

"What's the plan?" said Declan.

"We need to get the upper hand. But they all need to be together or it will complicate matters."

"They usually hang around the cabin until bedtime," said Declan. "If we hurry, we should be okay."

"When we get there, you'll go in first and make sure, then give me a sign."

"What sign?"

"Start whistling a tune. I'll be waiting in earshot."

Declan nodded and set off, silently leading the way

up the trail to the cabin.

† † †

Sdzeè shivered in the abandoned shack, cold and tired from the hike back. She decided a fire was in order—no way Declan was going to be looking for her tonight. The old barrel stove looked to be in working order, apart from the fact that the door latch was broken and had to be wired shut. She went outside and broke dead branches from the surrounding spruce trees. There was a stack of firewood outside, but it was rotten and mildewed from years of exposure to the elements.

The branches wouldn't burn long but would give her some warmth before she spent another restless night. After leaving Angel Creek, she thought about heading home, but it was too far and too late to attempt. *This will be my last night here*, she thought as she took a bite of the last bit of hardtack. She was nearly out of both food and patience. With the fire burning and warmth spreading throughout the shack, she lit the remnants of a candle found on the shelf beside the door and settled back against the bunk. From her pack she took the ragged journal from Heartbreak cabin, hoping to find a diversion in its pages.

She flipped slowly through the journal, filled with notes about the trapline, the weather, and other mundane thoughts. A tally of hides, marten and wolf, along with notes of disappointment about the low take. As the pages wore on, the disappointment grew. His wife was unhappy with life in the cramped cabin, miles from civilization. Summers were long, with little to do but try and raise a garden and put up stores for the winter. Sdzeè found he attempted to pan for gold, but with little success. She wondered if he knew what he was doing—unable to find gold in the middle of a rich district.

She continued flipping through the pages—the entries became shorter and more abrupt. Winter was approaching, the garden had largely failed, and his wife wanted to return to the home they left in Montana. Then the sickness struck—first the daughter, then the wife. He didn't know what to do to help them. He pondered going for help but didn't want to leave as they both sunk deeper into fever and labored breathing.

Sdzeè turned the page. It had one single entry, scrawled in the middle of the page:

```
Both passed this morning.
My heart is broken.
```

Sdzeè flipped through the remaining pages, but there was nothing further. No clue as to what happened to the trapper. She wondered if he stayed after burying his family—if he continued trapping or set out to return to civilization. *I will never know*, she thought as she closed the journal. But one thing was sure, those she loved would survive—she would see to that, and it would begin tomorrow.

† † †

Declan entered the cabin to find John and Emily sitting at the table, while Stella was finishing up dishes for the night.

"Have a nice walk?" said John. "You were gone for quite a while."

"It was okay," said Declan, still standing stiffly by the door. "Where's Thomas—in bed?"

"No, he went down to the sluice for a smoke or something, he should be back soon—why?"

Declan shifted his glance down to the dirt floor. "No reason—just wondering."

"Would you like some coffee?" said Stella. "There's a bit left from dinner."

"No thanks," said Declan. "Maybe I should go help Thomas."

"You're awfully eager tonight," said John, surprised at Declan's sudden acquisition of a work ethic.

Declan turned toward the door just as it opened. Thomas stood there, waiting for him to move. Declan stepped aside.

"Declan was worried about you," said John.

"Oh?"

Declan frowned. "No, just curious where everyone was."

Thomas took the last of the coffee and sat down at the table across from Emily. She got up and sat on the bunk. Declan remained near the door, his back against the wall. He started to whistle.

"You're sure acting strange tonight," said Thomas. "Why are you so—"

The door burst open, causing everyone except Declan to jump. Emily screamed, Thomas and John jumped up from the table, while Stella stood frozen. The figure at the door had a smile on his wrinkled face and a lever action rifle leveled at the two men.

Thomas glared. "What the—"

"Glad to see you all, folks. It's been a long time."

"Put the gun away," said John. "No need for that."

"Oh, I think there is."

Stella stared at the man. *There is something familiar about...*

"Hello, Stella. Don't you recognize me?"

Stella searched his face. *No, it couldn't be.* "Pierce?"

"Ah, you haven't forgotten me, love."

Thomas lunged forward, but John grabbed him.

"Easy, Tommy Boy, you wouldn't want me to have to shoot you—again," said Pierce.

Thomas was seething, the veins on his temple bulged as John struggled to restrain him. Emily was sobbing from the bunk, while Stella stood fixed on Pierce.

"Let's just have everyone sit down before someone gets hurt," said Pierce, gun still leveled directly at Thomas.

Stella sat down at the table and motioned for Thomas to do the same.

"What is going on?" said John, shooting a glance at Stella.

"Go ahead, Stella—tell 'em."

Stella hesitated. "This is Samuel Pierce, a longtime scoundrel and the man who shot Thomas the first day he arrived in Valdez."

Emily gasped while John shook his head in unbelief.

"What are you doing here?" said Thomas.

Pierce chuckled. "I've come to invest in your mine—well actually to take it from you."

"I swore if I ever saw you again, you'd pay for what you did to me," said Thomas.

"I think you're confused about who will be paying who."

John looked at Declan, now standing with his sidearm drawn. "What's your part in all this? How can you betray us after all we've done for you."

Declan just laughed and motioned to Pierce. "Fill them in."

Pierce nodded with a grin. "Folks, I'd like you to

meet my son, Cullen Pierce."

Stella gasped. "But the birth certificate—"

"Fake," said Cullen. "The whole story is phony and you dolts bought it hook, line, and sinker."

Stella jumped to her feet. "I knew my husband would never be unfaithful!"

"Sit down, love," said Pierce.

Thomas began to understand. It was all a con—a well conceived, intricate con. "When did this all begin?"

"Oh, that's the beauty of it Tommy Boy. I was sittin' fat and happy in Seattle when the newspapers starting gushing with news of a rich strike on Angel Creek and by golly if I didn't recognize my old friend's name."

"That's when we came up with the plan," said Cullen. "Pa knew enough about you, Stella, to put it all together."

"I still have some connections in Valdez, love. It was so easy to put it together, what with knowing you and your dear departed husband from my time there," said Pierce.

"You're lucky I'm not armed, or I'd shoot you dead in your tracks," said Thomas.

"Face it Tommy Boy—you're a loser. You were from the time I first met you on the steamer to Valdez. So naive—I knew you were an easy mark, I just didn't know you'd give me more than one payday."

Thomas was shaking—not from fear, but rage. He tried to see an out, but at the moment there was none. "What do you intend to do?"

"Well, you see that's an interesting question. We have a couple of options, but unfortunately, both of them end up with you being dead."

Emily was crying louder now, head in her hands.

"Oh, don't worry, my cute little thing," said Pierce.

"My boy Cullen here is kind of sweet on you—you might just come out of this unscathed, at least for a while."

Emily looked up, shock on her face. She looked to her father, then back at Cullen. He smiled at her and winked. She shook her head and looked away.

"You can't get away with this," said Thomas. "People around here know us."

"Oh, well Tommy Boy, you're just gonna get tired of mining and quit claim the deed over to me, then disappear."

"You're going to kill us—all of us?" said Stella. "Surely not even you can be that evil."

"Oh, you'll disappear all right, just like that Indian friend of yours," said Cullen.

Thomas jumped up from the table. "What do you know about that!" he said as John grabbed his arm.

Cullen just laughed. "Well, she was a little too nosy and caught me sampling the sluice box, so I just made her go away."

Thomas was breathing hard now, temples pounding. "You killed her? You bas—"

"Nah, I didn't kill her. I had her tied up in an old cabin next valley over and when I went back, she was gone—but since she hasn't come back, I figure a bear got her or she drowned or something. Either way, she got what she deserved."

Thomas slumped into the chair, the rage and stress finally taking its toll.

"Fetch the rope, boy," said Pierce. "We gotta tie these nice folks up until we decide the best way for them to disappear."

Cullen left the cabin for a moment, then returned with rope fetched from Pierce's horse. "Why not get it over with now?"

"Because, I'm tired from my long ride here, and we need to work out exactly how this will play out. Now tie them up."

Pierce kept the gun leveled while Cullen separated the men, then tied each up with their hands behind their back. Thomas wanted to lash out but couldn't see any way of getting the upper hand without one or more of them getting shot. Cullen moved to Stella and tied her up in the same fashion. He came to Emily, and tied her with her hands in front, then bent over and kissed her hard on the lips. She jerked her head away. John glared but didn't move.

Cullen laughed. "We'll continue that later, Em."

"Now, tie them all together and lash them to that bunk post," said Pierce.

Cullen finished the job, Stella, John, and Thomas sitting in chairs next to each other and Emily still on the bunk—all lashed together with a length of rope.

"Now what?" said Cullen.

"I'm going to get some sleep next door, and you're going to keep an eye on them. In the morning, we'll complete our little transaction and take out the garbage, so to speak."

"You won't get away with this Pierce," said Thomas.

"I already have."

† † †

CHAPTER 24

Thomas struggled against the ropes, succeeding in only making his wrists bleed even more. It was a fitful night, with little sleep for any of them. The first light of dawn peeked through the window, revealing Cullen, fast asleep in the chair by the door, rifle across his lap. Thomas motioned to John, who shook his head—it was pointless. Thomas seethed, unable to accept the situation. He never expected to see Pierce again, especially after moving north—yet here he was, ready to take it all.

Thomas leaned over and whispered to John, "We have to do something."

"I agree, but we have to wait for the right opportunity."

The door swung open, jolting Cullen awake. Pierce kicked the chair, nearly knocking it over. "Slacker, wake up."

Cullen growled. "Easy for you to say, you had a nice bed to sleep in."

Pierce just grinned. "How about some breakfast—a last meal so to speak."

"What do you intend to do with us?" demanded Thomas, his voice low.

"Well, Tommy Boy, first you're going to sign this quit claim deed, and then we'll talk about it," said Pierce as he pulled an envelope from his pocket.

"I'm not signing the claim over to you," said Thomas.

"You, will...if you want your lady folk to survive," said Pierce. "Or, we'll kill you all and forge your signature. Ain't nobody at the recorder's office in Eagle going to know the difference."

"Not even you can be that evil," said Stella. "You've done wrong, but I can't believe you would resort to this...to killing four people."

"Ah Stella, thank you for that, but you have no idea what I have done, or what I'm capable of."

"All for money," she said, shaking her head.

"What else is there?" said Pierce, poking Cullen in the arm, then laughing.

"You can't get away with it. Someone will find you out," said Thomas.

"Oh, we'll come up with a good story, cleanup your sluice, then make a quick sale and be gone. With those nuggets Cullen collected to show how rich the claim is, we should be able to get a tidy sum."

"Blood money," said John.

Pierce ignored him and motioned for Cullen to vacate the chair. He sat down and leaned back. "Cullen, untie Miss Stella there. I think she can be trusted to make us coffee and a nice breakfast."

Cullen untied Stella, then stepped back. She stood there, waiting.

"Now, get busy Stella, and don't think about pulling anything," said Pierce, waving his revolver. "I'd hate to see ole Tommy Boy or your new husband get a severe case of lead poisoning."

Stella got to work, stoking the wood stove, then getting the coffee on to boil. She started peeling potatoes, but worked slowly, hoping to forestall the inevitable. By the time the coffee was done, she had potatoes nearly ready for frying. She poured two cups, then gave them to Pierce and Cullen.

"Thanks," said Pierce. "You always were quite hospitable."

Stella didn't respond but poured three more cups of coffee. She sat two on the table and handed one to Emily, who grasped it with both hands. "How do you expect them to eat and drink with their hands tied behind their back?"

Pierce motioned to Cullen. "Tie them up with their hands in front. We want them to enjoy their last meal."

Cullen untied John first, Pierce keeping his revolver leveled at him the entire time. With John retied, Cullen moved to Thomas. There was a split instance of opportunity when his hands were free. He thought of overpowering Cullen and stood quickly. Cullen stepped back, nearly stumbling over the table as Thomas prepared to tackle him.

"Stop!" said Pierce. "Or Stella is going to regret it."

Thomas froze—the revolver was pointed at Stella's forehead, the hammer back and Pierce's finger on the trigger. Thomas slumped back into his chair and put his hands together. Cullen quickly tied them, reefing on them to make sure they were more than tight. Thomas winced in pain and pulled away.

"That ought to hold him," said Cullen, who started to turn away, then spun about, slugging Thomas in the jaw.

Emily screamed as Thomas groaned and slumped forward. "Stop, stop," she said between sobs.

"That's enough, Cullen. Relax," said Pierce.

Cullen took a seat and watched Stella as she finished preparing breakfast. She dished up two plates and sat them before Thomas and John.

"No, here," said Pierce. "We'll take those, and refill my coffee."

Stella obliged. "Are they allowed to eat?"

A sneer spread across Pierce's face. "Sure, just don't be too generous. I might want seconds."

Stella dished up two more plates and sat them on the table, then handed a plate to Emily.

"You're a real piece of work," said John.

Pierce waved the revolver at him. "Glad you think so. I try. Eat up, we have things to do today."

† † †

Sdzeè left the abandoned shack before dawn, making her way slowly toward Angel Creek. With no real plan, she hoped to arrive before the others were up and about. From there she would play it by ear, intending to somehow get the drop on Declan before he could react.

She thought about storming the cabin—bursting in with the Henry leveled, but there was no guarantee that he would be in the cabin. In order to prevent bloodshed, she first had to know where Declan was, and secondly, determine how to get the advantage.

As she trudged along, she mulled over her thoughts from the sleepless night before. The simplest plan—and one she rejected once already—was to just gun him down. Yet his crimes were minor thus far and given the justice of the land, she would be hard-pressed to prove his intentions. She would be a murderess and likely trotted off to the stockade at Fort Egbert in Eagle. The other option was to get the drop on him, then convince him she was crazy enough to shoot him so he would confess. *I can act crazy if I need to.*

A confession was the best possible outcome, but if need be, she could prove he was a thief by the bottle of nuggets tucked away in his pocket. Then there was the note, signed by someone named *S*—someone Declan was supposed to contact. She could only hope he hadn't done so yet. She was confident she could handle Declan—another person in the mix would severely complicate the situation.

She continued through the valley and began the climb that would take her to the ridge above Angel Creek. Though determined, she found herself shivering—and it wasn't from the cold. *I have to be careful. I have to be sure. Must not rush in.*

† † †

Pierce finished up his coffee, wiping his mouth with the back of his hand. "Let's get on with it," he said, waving the envelope, then placing it on the table. He removed a single sheet of paper, unfolded it, and pushed it toward Thomas.

"I'm not signing that," said Thomas.

Pierce stood, pulled his revolver from the holster, and pointed it at Stella's head. "You sure?"

John lunged forward, but the deafening sound stopped him short. He looked at Stella, still standing, still facing Pierce's revolver, then turned toward Cullen.

"That one went through the roof—next one goes through you," said Cullen, his revolver pointed squarely at John.

"Come on Tommy Boy. Be a good lad and just sign it. I'm sure John will be happy to oblige."

Thomas read the paper. It was a quit claim deed, assigning all rights to the claim to Cullen. "Why Cullen?"

"Well, Tommy Boy, I have a bit of a reputation. Cullen is still an unknown so it will be safer that way."

"You really think you can trust him?" said Thomas.

"Blood is blood, Tommy Boy—now sign," said Pierce, pushing a pencil across the table.

Thomas looked at John—John nodded. He picked up the pencil and started to sign, then stopped. "If we sign this there's nothing stopping you from killing us."

"Well, you're partially right. If you don't sign there's nothing stopping me from starting with Stella and sweet Emily here—and it will be long, slow, and painful, and you'll get to watch it all."

"You can't think you'll get away with it," said John. "You can't make four people just disappear, especially when people around here know us."

"Oh, I think we can. Cullen has told me about your other mine interest—the one with the nice sealed up drift where the Indian's husband lies. We'll just add a few more bodies to it and seal it back up. No one's going to go in there knowing it's a crypt."

Thomas knew there was no alternative but to sign—he believed the threat against Stella's life. His only hope was to somehow get the upper hand before it was too late. He signed the paper, then slid it over to John who did the same.

Pierce snatched up the paper, folded it, and put it in the envelope. "Thank you, now we can get on with the next order of business. Cullen, untie their feet so we can have a little walk."

Cullen obliged, then said, "Come on, up everybody. We're going down by the creek."

He herded the group out the door, Pierce following behind. They reached the creek and stopped at the water's edge. Emily was crying—the rest stood stiffly, waiting.

"I really hate to do this," said Pierce, "but there really is no other way."

"Liar! You are enjoying this," said Stella. "You have no conscience."

"Well, well, look who found her voice," said Pierce.

"Please, please, let us go," said Emily. "Declan, I thought you cared for me."

"The name is Cullen," he said, his face expressionless.

"I won't tell anyone if you let me go," said Emily. "We can be together."

Thomas turned, aghast at what he was hearing. Her true colors were bared to the world. He said nothing.

"Emily! I can't believe what you are saying," said her father.

"Not all of us have to die, Father. I would save you if I could. Cullen?"

Cullen smiled and looked at Pierce. "What do you think, Pa?"

"Well, she is pretty sweet—could be fun. Let's think about it," said Pierce. "But I think we'll start with sassy Miss Stella here. Cullen, you're on."

Cullen raised his revolver and put his thumb on the hammer to cock it. Out of the corner of his eye, he saw motion—Thomas, still bound, was rushing forward, head down.

Sdzeè descended the hill far below the Angel Creek claim and crossed the creek. Rather than hiding behind the outcrop again, she decided to cross over and work her way slowly up the trail toward the cabin. There was more cover along the way, and she hoped to get closer before confronting Declan. As she neared the cabin, she stepped off the trail and moved slowly through brush, weaving around the small stands of spruce.

Fifty yards from the cabin, she could see the door was standing open. She stopped and listened. Voices echoed up from the creek, just out of sight beyond the cabin. She moved closer, crouching below the window. Slowly she raised up to get a look—no one was inside. The voices got louder—she moved around the back side to get a view of the creek. She stifled a gasp at the sight.

Thomas, John, Stella, and Emily, all bound facing two men, both with guns. One was Declan—she didn't know the other. *This must be the mysterious man Declan sent the telegram to. This is a mess.*

She didn't know what to do. She could call out and try to distract them. She crouched lower and made her way to the corner of the cabin, straining to hear the conversation. To her horror, Declan raised his revolver—and Thomas charged forward.

† † †

Declan spun around and fired twice, missing Thomas who stumbled and hit the ground face first. Sdzeè didn't hesitate. She raised the Henry rifle and shot Declan through the chest. He took a step forward, then fell backwards into the creek, blood surging from the .44 caliber hole. Pierce already had his revolver up as he turned toward the cabin. Sdzeè fired again, hitting Pierce in the shoulder, spinning him around. He dropped his gun and Thomas scrambled forward to grab it.

Pierce was sitting on the ground, cradling his arm and groaning. "Don't move, Pierce," said Thomas, revolver leveled.

John picked up Cullen's gun and pointed it at him, but he wasn't moving, half-submerged in the creek.

Sdzeè sprinted down the hill to the creek. "Sdzeè! You're alive," said Thomas.

"Yes, but look!" she said, pointing behind them. There lay Emily, bleeding from her abdomen. With everyone focused on Cullen and Pierce, no one noticed she had been hit by one of Cullen's rounds.

Sdzeè quickly untied them and John and Stella rushed to Emily's side. Her eyes were open, but she was clearly in shock. Stella placed her hands on the wound to try and stop the bleeding while John held her hand.

Tears filled John's eyes. "How bad is it?"

Stella shook her head.

"Sdzeè, keep an eye on Pierce," said Thomas as he came over and knelt beside Emily. He looked at Stella. "We have to get help."

"Thomas, there's nothing we can do. She's losing too much blood."

Thomas cradled Emily's head, looking for some sign of recognition in her eyes. Her body spasmed and she coughed, blood seeping from the corners of her mouth. "Emily, stay with us," he said. She blinked, tried to speak, but could not. She let out a long gasp of breath, a rattle, and her eyes went blank.

Stella placed her hand on Thomas's arm. "She's gone, Thomas."

Despite all the adversity, he still cared for her. He looked at her, tears welling up in his eyes. What might have been flashed through his mind, then anger filled him. He stood and walked over to Pierce. "This is all your fault," he said as he raised the revolver and placed it to his forehead. Pierce stared at him, gun pressed hard into his flesh.

"Now you're going to pay for all you've done—to me—to my friends," said Thomas as he drew back the hammer.

He felt a hand on his arm and looked. It was Sdzeè. She gently lowered his arm. "Thomas, it is not worth it. Do not become like him. You are a good man."

Thomas looked at John in his grief, Stella hugging him to try and bring comfort. He held back his emotions as he looked at Pierce, bleeding slightly from his shoulder wound. "Turn about is fair play it seems," said Thomas.

"I guess you got even for me shooting you," said Pierce.

Thomas shoved him to the ground, Pierce groaning as Thomas rolled him over and tied his hands behind his back. "We're not anywhere close to even, Pierce. We're turning you over to the military in Eagle. They can deal with you."

Pierce laughed through the pain. "I've done nothing. Nothing you can pin on me anyway."

"Don't you even care about your dead son and all the pain you've caused?"

"Cullen meant no more to me than my revolver—just a tool to use to accomplish what I want."

"You truly are evil," said Thomas as he rolled him back over and ripped the envelope from his pocket. "I'll take this," he said.

Pierce growled but said nothing.

Thomas motioned to Sdzeè. "Help me drag Declan out of the creek."

Declan's head was underwater, his feet near the bank. He was obviously dead. Thomas and Sdzeè dragged him out of the water. Thomas searched his pockets, finding the small bottle nearly filled with gold nuggets. He reached into a small pocket inside Declan's vest and pulled out a chain—a chain with an old pocket watch attached. He held it up high. "Stella."

She looked, then tears filled her eyes as she rushed to take the watch from Thomas. The depth of Declan's deception saddened her as she clutched the watch tightly.

Thomas motioned to John who was still kneeling next to his daughter. "Come, let's take care of Emily. I'll get the wagon so we can bring her up to the cabin," said Thomas. John nodded, tears running down his face and still shaking as Stella moved to support him.

Thomas turned to Sdzeè. "Thank you. You've saved my life again."

"I am sorry about Emily. I wish I could have stopped all of it."

"You did all you could—I'm glad you showed up when you did. Where have you been?"

Sdzeè took his hand, compassion flooding her face. "I will tell you all about it—someday.

EPILOGUE

The late summer days grew shorter as the fireweed finished blooming, a sure sign of the impending fall. Already the birch leaves had taken a hint of gold. Soon the sandhill cranes would be heard far overhead, their distinct voices in chorus as they flew south. There was so much to do before the first snow, when the land fell silent for the long winter.

Thomas surveyed the stack of split firewood, trying to decide if it was enough. As he put another log on the splitting block, his mind drifted to the events of the spring. The death of Emily was hard on them, but more so on John. He and Stella, after much debate, decided to return to Valdez, to reopen her boarding house and make a life there. To remain would have been a constant reminder of his loss, something John couldn't face.

Sdzeè's cabin was larger and better suited for the winter—they had moved their shortly after John and Stella departed. Thomas swung the axe and split the spruce log. As he picked it up, the glint of the gold band caught his eye. *Funny how things don't go the way you plan,* he thought as he spun the ring on his finger.

Sdzeè was strong, brave, and so much more. She saved him—saved them all, and he could never thank her enough.

The cabin door opened and there, with a cup of coffee in her hand and grin on her face, was his wife. Thomas looked at her—and smiled.

GLOSSARY OF TERMS

This is a glossary of mining and other terms used in the book. For some terms there may be more than one definition, but the one provided here is in the historical context of the story.

bench: A terrace on the side of a stream

cheechako: A person newly arrived in Alaska or one inexperienced in the ways of life in the far north

collar: The opening of a shaft

concentrate: Fine gravel, sand, and magnetite recovered from a sluice box and further processed to recover the gold

cribbing: Timbers constructed at right angles to each other to support a shaft

drift: A horizontal underground working in a mine.

dump: See *winter dump*

headframe: A framework above a mine shaft, used to support hoisting

magnetite: A black magnetic mineral commonly found in placer deposits. Also known as "black sand".

placer: A gold deposit found in recent or ancient stream gravels

siwash: Camp outdoors without a tent or shelter

sluice box: A wooden box with riffles used to process gravel and capture gold.

sluicing: Running gravel through a sluice box to recover gold

shaft: A vertical mine working that provides underground access, usually timbered for support.

shoh: Bear

stockpile: A pile of gravel waiting to be processed (sluiced) to recover gold

tsaan: Dung

ts'olnüüdn: Devil

udzih: Caribou

wing dam: An angled dam in a creek used to increase water flow.

winter dump: Material excavated from an underground drift mine during the winter and stockpiled for sluicing during the summer.

xaiy eek: Parka

ABOUT THE AUTHOR

G.E. Sherman has a wide and varied background, including that of geologist, mining engineer, software engineer, and author. He has authored both technical books and articles, as well as fiction. In addition to being the founder of the popular open source QGIS project, he has published a number of books on the topic.

When writing fiction, he draws on the depth of his background, providing vivid descriptions of life on the last frontier, wildlife encounters, and survival. Further, his experience as an outdoor enthusiast provides inspiration in the stories he tells.

G.E. Sherman resides in Alaska and regularly watches moose from his living room window.